Sexual
Wishes
Sexy
Stories
Collection

VOLUME 12

10 EROTIC SHORT STORIES

GARRETT ZEIGER

Sexual Wishes/ Garrett Zeiger. -- 1st ed.
Xplicit Press, an imprint of TLM Media LLC

ISBN-13: 978-1-62327-543-3
ISBN-10: 1-62327-543-1
eISBN: 978-1-62327-593-8

Printed in the United States of America

CONTENTS

1 SUCKING THE SUCCUBUS

Jonathan grew up hearing tales of the succubus Crysteel - whispered stories told behind the old mill when the adults were too busy to monitor their teenage children. Crysteel was a devilish strumpet with tits the size of melons, who just loved to suck dick. They said she sucked out your soul while she sucked you off - but at least you died happy and hard.

When Marcus made that joke the first time, Jonathan punched him in the shoulder. He'd laughed, thinking how true it was he'd like to die with a hard-on, having just had his cock licked by a dirty slut – the kind of slut only a succubus could be.

They said Crysteel would come to you in your sleep. You'd be dreaming about your wife or girlfriend, but it would be Crysteel who unbuttoned your trousers. She would stroke your cock to attention, licking your balls while she got your dick wet with her tongue.

You might wake up because you'd get so big, with your balls screaming for release. But by then it would be too late. Her hand and mouth on your cock would be too much to withstand. You'd look down and see her slender shoulders, hunched over the work she'd be doing with her ruby lips, and before you knew it, you'd shoot cum so hard your soul would come out with your semen.

Then you'd become an undead sex slave, doomed to pleasure Crysteel however she wished for all eternity.

But those were just stories, and Jonathan was grown up, now. Married, with a child on the way, he worked most days plowing the fields, and most nights plowing his wife. He was happy enough, and yet... every so often he found himself recalling those tawdry tales of Crysteel the succubus. They always brought a smile to his face, and a little dribble to the tip of his dick.

Myra, Jonathan's wife, was three months pregnant with their first child and just beginning to show. Her tits weren't changing much, but since they were already hefty handfuls, Jonathan loved to play with them any way he could. He particularly liked to suck them, getting a taste of what the baby would be enjoying. Then he'd have Myra bunch them up together so he could shove his hard cock in between and fuck her there. The tip of his dick would slide up and down through her tits until he shot cum all over her pale, freckled throat.

Those were just Myra's tits, to say nothing of her cunt and ass.

But Myra, dealing with the effects of pregnancy, was practically frigid. She rarely initiated sex anymore, and was even refusing to take it up the ass. Jonathan found himself dreaming of sex more than actually having it. He dreamed of Crysteel, the fabled succubus he'd first heard about so many years ago.

His dreams were vague and indistinct. In them Crysteel was

nothing more than a dark apparition that would coalesce about his hips and nudge him until he got hard. The dreams became more intense, however, especially as Myra's sleep patterns began to change.

It was really weird, but for some reason Myra couldn't sleep at night. She kept having bad dreams that woke her up, so she took to knitting by the fire until dawn. Only then was she able to get some shuteye, while Jonathan was out working in the fields.

As a result, Jonathan often found himself sleeping alone after a hearty dinner, with nothing more than a peck on the cheek from his wife to get him through the night. So even though it was a soul-sucking succubus he dreamed of, Jonathan looked forward to his nighttime visions. After all, they were harmless enough... right?

One night Jonathan dreamed of Crysteel, and she spoke to him for the first time. "You've been calling me for weeks, you little horn dog. You don't think I'm real, but tomorrow night I will come to your bed and show you just how real I truly am. And I will suck your soul into Hell!"

Startled, Jonathan awoke. Once again he was hard, but that quickly subsided thanks to the fear. He rubbed his fingers over his close cut head of hair and blinked. Here he was, a grown man with a beautiful (if unaffectionate) wife, a fine little hut of a home, and a new child on the way. Why should he be having nightmares like these? And yet...

He could feel Crysteel's ruby lips kissing the head of his cock, as if she were real.

Concerned for the safety of his family, Jonathan decided to see the village priest before leaving for the fields. He walked across the village and knocked on the wooden door of the tiny church there. "Father," he said, "I've been having evil dreams. I fear I am being visited by a succubus! Can you protect me?"

The old priest, a white haired man wearing gray robes and carrying a cane, peered out the door. "Ah, my child, a succubus is a dangerous creature. The best way to protect you is to cast out all impure thoughts!"

Jonathan's face fell.

"But, if that cannot be done... Here! Take this." The priest reached into his robes and pulled out a crystal vial. "Drink this with your dinner tonight, and Godspeed!"

Jonathan looked at the vial filled with purple liquid and asked, "What is it, Father?"

"Nothing I may tell you of, my son. Go, take it on faith, and do not tell anyone you have done so." Then he closed the door of the church.

Jonathan carefully placed the vial in his satchel and went to work for the day.

When he returned home after a long day of hard work, Jonathan ate a hearty meal made by Myra. He washed the contents of the vial down with a big swig of milk when she wasn't looking, then threw the vial out the window. As he drank it all – the potion being very bitter – he felt a sensation in his balls, like they had become tight with invisible armor of some kind. It was very strange indeed.

The evening was not much of

anything, as Jonathan was winding down from his day, and Myra was just getting started with her knitting. Soon enough, Jonathan felt tired and rolled into the small bedroom to lie down. He lay on the mat under the covers, surprised that he could still feel the effect of the potion the priest had given him.

Soon enough, he fell asleep and entered dreamland.

Once again he dreamed he felt a nudging against his balls. His dream eyes opened to see a dark mist hovering above him. There flickered in the mist near his face two pinpricks of light, like cat's eyes. The blanket had been pulled aside to reveal his limp dick. But it did not stay limp for long. A spectral hand cupped and prodded until he became erect. Then the hand stroked his cock nice and slow, all the way from the base of his balls to the moistening tip.

Then those ruby lips appeared,

kissing the head of his cock a little before parting wide to let it all in. Jonathan felt Crysteel's tongue slide along his shaft, and then the head of his cock dipped down her throat, all the way down until she was kissing his substantial balls. She choked a bit, his size so great, and then she started seriously sucking.

As she sucked his dick, her body began to take form. Soon enough, Jonathan could see her demon-red flesh and raven-black hair. She had two little horns poking out of the top of her head, which bobbed up and down over his dick, faster and faster. Then her great leathery wings appeared, fanning up above them both. Her face, when she looked up from the work she was doing with her mouth, was sharp yet beautiful. Rich, like the color of blood, her teeth sharp white crystals. And yet she sucked dick smooth and hard, better than any whore.

Crysteel took her left hand and jostled Jonathan's balls as she resumed sucking. She laughed a little, anticipating his coming, but no matter how fast she slid her lips back and forth along the considerable length of his dick, she couldn't make him cum. She jostled his balls a second time. She nibbled lightly at the tip of his dick.

While this was going on, Jonathan realized he was no longer sleeping... and no longer dreaming! There really was a hot and horny demon giving him head in bed, with his wife in the room next door! He thought about yelling for help, but quickly changed his mind when he noticed just how good all of this felt. Here he was, getting the blowjob of a lifetime, and if he looked down he could see Crysteel's melon tits swinging and swaying with the motion, and her plump round ass tilted up behind it all.

Not only this, but Jonathan suddenly became aware of something very special. He was in complete control of when he was going to cum. The potion he had swallowed guaranteed that he would not come until he consciously chose to do so. And, since the succubus Crysteel meant to steal his soul with his semen, he decided to give her neither.

So, she sucked and sucked. Although his dick remained huge and ready, he did not cum. Finally, tired, the succubus looked up in frustration and whispered, "What the fuck? How can you not cum?"

Jonathan smiled. "Maybe I need to see more of your body."

Crysteel huffed in disbelief, but then obliged. "Okay darling. How's this?" She stood up and squatted down over Jonathan's face, showing him up close and personal just how beautiful her swollen pussy lips and puckered asshole could be. "I'll have sex with you... on one condition. You must come in my mouth before dawn, and nowhere else. Mouth only!" she repeated, pointing with graceful red fingers at her ruby red lips.

"Fine. But why don't you have a seat... for now?"

Crysteel giggled and lowered herself, letting Jonathan lap at her cunt and asshole. He stuck his tongue up her ass and then lapped her all the way from rectum to clit. He loved the taste of her, like sour candy. She moaned.

Then Jonathan pushed her up and back.

Obediently, Crysteel the succubus pushed her pussy lips against the head of his enormous shaft. She had to steady herself, backing down on top of him, taking him in slowly.

Jonathan marveled at her gorgeous breasts and flowing hair as he felt himself slide up and inside. He watched as she found her rhythm, bouncing up and down on his cock, and she seemed not so resentful now. She actually seemed to be enjoying things, what with stuffing herself full of dick. When Jonathan reached up and grabbed her swaying tits and rubbed her dark nipples between his fingers, he got a reaction.

Crysteel shuddered. "Oh, God!" she said, a little too loudly.

"Shhhh!!!!" said Jonathan, holding a warning finger up to his lips.

"Sorry," she whispered.

Something had obviously begun to change in this little relationship. Jonathan wondered what he might do next.

His unspoken question was answered soon enough, when Crysteel lay down on her side and raised her leg. Then she grabbed her ass cheek and pulled it up, showing off her tight little asshole. "Fuck me here, now," she said, making a wink.

Jonathan was happy to oblige. He stood up and coaxed her onto her hands and knees. Then he pressed her head down on the sleeping mat, her black locks flowing over her horns and face. Next he moved her legs forward so her ass was up between her wings and ready to receive every inch of his cock.

Happy to be in this position, Crysteel spread her ass cheeks wide. "Fuck that ass, master." she whispered.

Jonathan pressed the head of his cock against her puckered sphincter. It looked almost too big to fit inside, but it did, with some spit and steady insertion.

"Oh," she said, "that feels wonderful."

Jonathan slid in deeper, and then pulled back a bit before going even deeper. Slowly, he worked her until she was ready for some seriously deep ass drilling. Then it was in and out, in and out, her asshole open wide and flexing with each thrust. He even pulled completely out a few times, to see her gape there, then shoved it back in for more. Pumping and pumping, she loved getting fucked up the ass by his big dick.

And then he decided something. He would cum but not in her mouth. Instead, he shot his hot load all up in the depths of her rectum.

When she felt the warm rush of cum deep inside, Crysteel cried out in ecstasy and frustration. "Damn you!" she cried. "Now I am yours... forever!" She rolled over, cum dripping from her asshole. She rubbed herself there, getting ass juice and cum all over her fingers. Then she put them in her mouth and swallowed all the wetness down.

Jonathan felt something snap inside. He knew he had control over Crysteel now. And when Myra called from the other room regarding the noise, he yelled back, "Nothing, dear!" Then he motioned for Crysteel to fly out the window. "I'll summon you when I need you."

Crysteel obeyed, and Jonathan had a good night's sleep.

2 SHARING THE SUCCUBUS
Sucking The Succubus Part 2

Tonight was just another typical night for Jonathan. The Crysteel, the sexy succubus now under his control, was once again giving him head in the bedroom while his wife Myra – thinking him asleep – was knitting in the main living room of their small cottage in the village. It had been great fun, having furtive sexual encounters with Crysteel whenever he wished. She let him do things to her his wife hardly ever allowed, especially now that his wife was pregnant. While Myra never asked for anything in bed anymore, Crysteel was always ready to suck dick and be ass-fucked in every imaginable way.

Still, because Myra slept during the days when Jonathan was working in the fields, and then stayed up all night knitting while Jonathan slept (after having quiet sex with Crysteel, who flew in through the bedroom window); they began to miss each other. In particular, Jonathan missed Myra's big pregnant tits and her round ass. Jonathan was sure Myra still had some sexual desire; that she had to be rubbing herself to orgasm after he left for work every day. He just needed to figure out a way to get her interested in sex again.

"Master," said Crysteel, popping Jonathan's dick out of her mouth with a sloppy sucking sound, "Where are you? Your mind seems far away."

"It is, Crysteel," he whispered.

"Is there something I'm not doing? Should I suck harder? Would you like to fuck me in the ass now?"

"No. No, Crysteel. I am thinking of my wife, Myra."

Crysteel's big black wings twitched. "Oh! And I suppose you'd rather be fucking her pregnant ass instead of mine?"

"No, Crysteel. Not instead, together. I want to have sex with both of you at the same time."

"Oh. Well, I don't really want that... and I doubt she does either." She kissed the head of Jonathan's cock with her ruby lips, and then smiled with her sharp white teeth.

"You know, Crysteel. It would be in your best interest to seduce my wife."

"Oh?" She quickly fluttered her tongue all along his shaft, from top to bottom and back again. "Why?"

"Because," and now Jonathan was creatively lying, "if you can bring her to orgasm with your tongue, then you will have control over her child, which will be a boy."

"Hmm... that does sound tempting. But why would you allow me to possess the soul of your child?"

"Because I possess your soul, my dear. Which means you may never do anything I don't allow you to do."

"Oh." Crysteel turned on her other side and spread her ass cheeks. "Fuck my ass, my master, and I will think about what you are suggesting."

Jonathan grinned, seeing how well this could work out for all three of them. But for now, he had simply to shove his big dick up Crysteel's puckered asshole to keep her satisfied.

When Jonathan woke up the next morning, Myra made him breakfast. She looked tired. While he ate, she sat down next to him and said, "My love."

"Yes?"

"Would you like to fuck me this morning before you leave for work?" She twirled a stray bit of dark hair hanging in her face.

"What, my darling?"

"Well, we haven't had sex for a couple of months now. It must be hard on you."

"It's not the best, Myra. But I only want you to have sex with me if that is what you want." Jonathan saw his wife tense when he said that.

"Jonathan."

"Yes?"

"Are you sure you're not fucking some young hussy behind my back?"

"Whoa! Myra, absolutely not!"

Jonathan slapped his hands down on the kitchen table. "If you want me to fuck you, just say so!"

"But –"

Jonathan interrupted her with a passionate kiss. He then quickly lifted her skirt from behind and gently bent her pregnant body over the kitchen table. Supporting herself with both arms, she kept the pressure off her belly while offering her backside up for penetration.

After rubbing Myra's pussy with his fingertips until she started to get wet, Jonathan slid his dick into her snatch from behind. It felt good to be back in his wife's pussy, and he almost shot his load before she reached orgasm herself. But he relaxed and held back, timing it just right so that she did get to appreciate his dick before he spit cum in her cunt.

"Now," said Jonathan sternly, "No more talk of hussies. When you want a good fucking, talk to me, instead of knitting all night and sleeping all day."

He then left the cottage to go work in the fields.

That evening, when Jonathan returned home from the fields, he found his wife sitting in the living room. She was awake, but looking very sleepy. Concerned for her and her baby, Jonathan asked, "Are you all right?"

"Yes, Jonathan," she yawned. "I just tried to stay awake all day so we could sleep together tonight." She flashed a pretty smile.

This warmed Jonathan's heart, so he cooked dinner that night and they went to bed early. Only, Myra was too tired to want to have sex. This was fine by Jonathan, as he had plans for later...

There came the flapping of wings at the window, and Crysteel sat on the sill, crouching naked with the moonlight shining on the demon-red skin of her bum. "Master," she whispered.

Jonathan got up from the bed, careful not to wake his wife. "We need to change our routine this night," he said quietly to his servant of a succubus. "My wife is sleeping in our bed tonight."

Crysteel angrily pouted but did not make a sound.

"Here's what I want you to do..." He then proceeded to detail what was to happen. After he finished his careful instructions, he looked Crysteel in the eye and said "Okay? Are you ready?"

Crysteel smiled and licked her lips. She nodded in agreement.

Jonathan gave her a wink. Then he stood away from the window to allow Crysteel to enter and begin working her sexual magic.

It was a warm night, so it was safe for Crysteel to pull the covers away from Myra's pregnant body. She lay on her back, wearing a loose slip of a nightgown that covered very little. In fact, with her legs bent upward at the knees, it was easy to see her naked cunt between her legs, and one of her large breasts had rolled out the side of her top. She was beautiful, sleeping there with her full tummy like a little world all too itself in the middle of her body.

Not yet ready to awaken her master's wife, Crysteel kept very quiet as she crouched down between Myra's legs.

Slowly, she inhaled the feminine scent of her and then blew gently there, letting the little gusts of her breath move Myra's pubic hair just the slightest bit and give just the faintest stroke of airy pressure against her clit. Myra moved just a little, and then Crysteel blew harder one last time upon that nodule of pleasure just above her pussy.

Now Crysteel licked her there, very softly, and felt her clit stiffen up. Then she licked lower, along her pussy lips, which started to unfold. Still asleep, Myra was breathing deeply and making little sounds of enjoyment. Soon Crysteel was lapping up the juices of Myra's beautiful flower of a cunt, and bringing her ever closer to a waking state of arousal.

As this critical point in time drew near, Jonathan lay down next to his wife and began softly kissing her face. Still asleep, Myra kissed him back.

Crysteel reached up with her hands to spread Myra's thighs and ass cheeks open wide, as she continued to lick her cunt. She knew Myra would soon climax, so she spit on her asshole and began licking there as well. Then she straightened her tongue and used it to give Myra a shallow fucking in her cunt, while her nose bumped up against her clit.

"I have someone to share with you, my dear," whispered Jonathan in his wife's ear.

At that moment Myra shook with her orgasm. Her entire body quivered in ecstasy as her husband kissed her hard on her mouth, and Crysteel did the same on her cunt.

"Oh! Jonathan!" Myra was awake now, but she did not yet realize there was a second person in bed with her besides Jonathan.

"Myra," he said. "I want you to meet Crysteel."

At that moment, the succubus popped her head up over Myra's pregnant belly with a devilish grin. Her sharp white teeth and sparkling red eyes glowed in the moonlight coming through the window.

Myra started to scream, but Jonathan shushed her with kisses. "I'm sorry to spring her on you like this, but I thought it best you two meet."

"Who is she? What is she?"

"She is a succubus, my love. Her name is Crysteel, and she is my slave. The priest of our church told me how to control her, and now she does my bidding."

"And you've been having sex with her, in this very bed?"

"Well," said Jonathan, afraid his plan was falling apart, "So have you, now."

"I –" But Myra could think of nothing more to say. She fell silent.

Then Crysteel spoke. "Do not blame your husband. I came to him the first time with every intention of stealing his soul. But, somehow, he overcame my advances. He did the stealing instead of me. He stole my heart."

Myra found the voice of the succubus difficult to resist, as it was now magically associated in her very being with the tremendous orgasm she had just experienced. She remained silent, unable to stop thinking about sex: sex with Jonathan, sex with Crysteel, sex with anyone at all!

After a few difficult moments, Jonathan quietly asked, "How are you feeling, my love?"

"Come here!" said Myra, to Crysteel.

To everyone's surprise, Crysteel immediately obeyed, quickly crawling around to bring face close to Myra's.

"I feel something. You are mine now, too, aren't you?"

The succubus blinked. She started to say something, and then blinked again. "My God!" she shouted. "You tricked me!" She looked accusingly at Jonathan. "You promised me her baby's soul, but now I have two masters instead of just one!"

Myra laughed. "Oh, my. Here we have my husband thinking I did not notice that he was fucking a succubus in our bedroom. And here we have this succubus, thinking she could take advantage of me. I've been aware of things all along! Hahahahaha."

Jonathan looked dumbfounded, and Crysteel was simply pursing her ruby lips in a pout.

"Now, let's have a good threesome we can all enjoy, shall we?" Myra massaged her heavy tits and then looked down at them suggestively.

Jonathan kissed her right nipple, while Crysteel kissed her left.

"There we go. After this I think I should like Crysteel to eat me out a second time, while my husband fucks her hard in the ass."

Neither of the two supplicants on her tits said anything to disagree.

"Good. Then it's decided." Myra watched as her husband and the succubus sucked her nipples and smeared saliva all over her big tits.

Finally, Jonathan moved closer and kissed Crysteel. This broke the mood of that particular position. So, Crysteel crawled around to Myra's dripping cunt, her red ass raised up under her black wings for Jonathan's advantage.

With Crysteel's face buried in his wife's pussy, Jonathan grabbed both ass cheeks of the succubus and spread them wide apart. Her demon twat and puckered asshole revealed themselves for the taking, so he spit on the tip of his dick and slid it deep in between her pussy lips. Then he took his right thumb and rubbed some more spit around her tight little sphincter, circling his way in until he was two joints deep. Plugging her asshole with his thumb, he started pumping her pussy with his big, thick cock. This caused her to bounce against him, and her head to press in and out against

Myra's hungry twat.

"Eat my cunt, you demon whore!" shouted Myra, moaning loudly with the sensation of Crysteel's tongue inside her. "I'm going to cum again, and when I do, he's going to fuck your ass harder than it's ever been fucked before."

Even Crysteel moaned at the thought of this, and at the way Jonathan was filling her cunt.

Soon enough, Myra shivered all over a second time.

On cue, Jonathan pulled his thumb out of Crysteel's asshole. It stayed open, gaping black and red for his cock to come inside next. With the length of his shaft covered in pussy juice, he buried it deep in her ass.

She moaned loudly. "Yes! Fuck me hard, master!"

Jonathan than grabbed her ass cheeks with both hands and pounded her little asshole. It stretched and flexed, eager to receive every inch of his hard penetration.

While her husband ass-fucked their succubus slave, Myra got up and came to squat behind Jonathan. She saw his ass cheeks pivot and sway as he pumped Crysteel with his cock. Then she reached between his legs and grabbed his balls, squeezing them.

"Oh! Fuck yes!" cried Jonathan. Feeling the blood fill every vein in his cock, he knew the head of his dick was huge as it pulled all the way out of Crysteel's gaping asshole and dove straight back in, over and over. Soon enough, he felt a stirring in his balls, and he shot what felt like a never-ending stream of cum deep up inside the succubus' bouncing ass. He felt cum drip out of her hole and off his balls as he kept fucking her.

Then Myra pulled him away. She kissed and licked Crysteel's wet butthole, then swallowed her husband's dirty dick.

Crysteel reached behind herself and wet her fingers in her ass so she could taste it.

And Jonathan, barely able to remain standing after cumming so hard, pressed his hand against the side of Myra's head as he thought; "Now that was fun!"

3 WHORING THE VILLAGE
Sucking The Succubus Part 3

The widowed leader of the village, Patrick, lived in a nicely constructed tower overlooking the homes of his subjects on one side and their farmland on the other. It was another uneventful evening for him, as he finished his late supper and wiped his graying beard. Setting down his napkin, he called for the servant girl to remove his dishes. "Donna!" he called licking his lips. The stew had been particularly good.

Within moments, Donna – quiet and politely shy – bustled into the dining room. She wore a tightly fitted yellow apron over her light brown gown. She was the only servant he had kept on after the passing of his beloved wife, Amanda. Wearing her hair in a russet bob, she craned her smooth-skinned neck as she bent down to gather Patrick's cup and bowl. "My Lord," she said, as the curtsied and turned round and headed back into the kitchen.

Patrick eyed the pert mound of her backside underneath her clothing as she departed. It was a shame he had not seen more of her lovely body, but for some reason he still felt uncomfortable with even the notion of approaching her. She was ripe, and probably ready, but something in his mind stayed his advances.

When he retired that night, he thought of Donna before fading away into slumber...

In his dreams, Donna crept naked into his bedchamber and pulled aside his blankets. In the moonlight through the window, he could just make out her tiny breasts and cherry nipples.

Pressing her hand against his hardening cock, she massaged it through the thin silk of his sleeping gown until he had a mighty erection. Then she lifted his gown to expose his ready cock. Craning her delicate neck once again, she bent down and began stroking him with her tongue. She wiggled the tip of her tongue between his balls before sliding up along his shaft and nibbling at the head of his dick.

He dribbled pre-cum, which she delicately licked away. Softly moaning now, he begged her to suck him off.

She obliged, hungrily swallowing the head of his penis in her mouth and whirling circles around it with her tongue. Then she swallowed his entire length, down to his balls. She held his cock in her throat a moment, before raising her head and then rapidly sucking him off with rapid up and down motion.

He was in awe at her skill, and when she grabbed his balls and squeezed, he felt his cum ready. A great wave of pleasure started at the base of his cock and rumbled up its length, until he shot his load into her open mouth.

When this happened, he suddenly awoke, realizing that someone was indeed sucking his cock. But it was not Donna.

Instead, he saw above him a

gorgeous woman with blazing red hair and two little red horns sticking out the top of her head. Looking down lower, he saw that her tits were like two magnificent melons.

Two candles illuminated the room, revealing her skin to be a sweet alabaster. When he looked into her dazzling eyes, he was completely intoxicated with her beauty. "I am yours," he said... and after he said these words, he wondered who had spoken them.

"Yes you are, my Patrick, my slave." She then rolled over in the bed beside him. "Now, it is your task to give me oral pleasure. I want you to lick my cunt and asshole until I tell you to stop."

Unable to resist her command, Patrick got up and kneeled so that he could position his bearded mouth in the requested places. Soon he was licking and sucking the twin holes between her spread legs. As he nuzzled her clit with his nose and dipped his tongue into her anus, he noticed something amazing.

The devil woman in his bed began to transform. First, he noticed a long red and pointy tail now attached to her backside underneath her puckered asshole. Then he watched as her supple flesh – all over her attractive body – turned from pale to deep russet, like Donna's hair. As she started to come, she even sprouted large black wings, which unfurled beneath the back on which she lay.

Finally, she clutched his graying head of hair and purred with orgasm. "Ah! That's how you do it, Patrick. Now, allow me to introduce you to our little family…"

When Patrick stepped into the entry hall of his tower behind the succubus that had entranced him, he did not know what to expect. He was understandably surprised to find the chamber well lit with candles. But what was even more surprising was the presence of a man and a woman. He recognized them from the village. The man was Jonathan, a competent farmer dressed in a long dark-brown cloak, and the woman was his lovely wife Myra, whose breasts and pregnant belly pressed against her simple blue evening gown.

"I think you know these two, Patrick," said the succubus. "My name, by the way, is Crysteel." The sultry devil-woman then walked over to Jonathan and gave him a long, wet kiss.

"Wha –" began Patrick, but then he lost all words when he saw Donna enter the room from a side passage.

She was naked from head to toe, like in his dream, her soft bare feet treading lightly on the floor of stone. The hair above her dangling pussy lips was the same color as the russet hair on her head. In both hands she carried a short thin dildo, which she held up on display for Myra and Jonathan to see. "Will this do?" she asked.

"Let's find out," said Jonathan. He took the dildo from her and slapped it against the servant girl's pert little ass. "Why don't you get down on the floor so we can see?"

Without further words, Donna bent over, touching her toes and then holding her ankles with her hands, leaving her pussy and asshole well exposed.

Jonathan fondled her there then spit on the dildo before using it to move her longish pussy lips from side to side. He slid the dildo all along her young slit before penetrating her pink pussy hole.

Donna squealed delightfully, inviting Jonathan to plunge the dildo in and out of her tight twat over and over.

While this was going on, Myra moved gracefully in front of Patrick. "Did you enjoy Crysteel, my lord?"

Patrick sputtered, "Of course! But..." His words trailed off as he watched Jonathan fuck Donna with the dildo.

"Let me explain what is going to happen."

"Please do."

"You have experienced the orgasm of your life, courtesy of the Succubus Crysteel. Now, you are her slave. And, since she is our slave, you are ours as well."

Patrick wanted to resist, but found Myra's appearance all too lovely. Her dark head of hair was healthy and long, flowing down to good-sized breasts above a tummy he found unusually appealing. He imagined its taut roundness above her well-used cunt and felt himself growing hard.

Crysteel, with her dark-red skin and black wings, had even bigger tits with bulging nipples. As she walked by Patrick, he remembered the feel of her sucking his cock, and also the taste of her nether regions. Everyone here was gorgeous in his/her own way, and Patrick realized he would do anything for any of them.

"Let's start you out a little slow, shall we?" Myra hiked up her blue gown in front, presenting her flat pussy for Patrick's enjoyment. "Lick me."

Patrick dropped to his knees. He inhaled the moist scent of her through his nose and then licked all along her already dripping twat.

Meanwhile, Crysteel moved beside Myra and started tongue-kissing her.

In the background, they could all three hear Donna's moans and the sounds of encouragement made by Jonathan. "Oh. Oh yes! Slide it in my asshole, too!"

As Patrick lapped like a thirsty dog at the pussy juices of pregnant Myra, he pulled away his nightgown completely.

Following suit, Myra and Jonathan also disrobed. Then, all five of them were naked and ready to fuck.

"Patrick," said Jonathan, "I think your little servant girl here is ready for your dick."

Eager to taste this sweetest that had always been so close to him these many months, Patrick raced to stand in front of Donna, who was now on her knees, ready to receive his cock in her mouth.

She sucked him well, rapidly stroking his shaft with her hand while kissing with little slurping sounds the tip of his dick.

Myra and Crysteel entertained each other nearby, while Jonathan fondled himself and enjoyed the show.

When Patrick had had enough of Donna's mouth, he pulled her up by the hair of her head. "You beautiful slut," he whispered in her ear. Then he embraced her, lifting her up off the ground and onto his cock, which slid past her dangling pussy lips and into her tight little pink hole with a wet slurping noise.

No longer wishing to just watch, Jonathan took up the position behind Donna, angling her so that he could slide his heft dick straight up her even tighter asshole.

Feeling the pressure of two cocks inside her at one time, Donna let out an ecstatic yelp. She bounced up and down on both shafts, their bulbous ends pounding her deep inside.

While still fucking his servant girl, Patrick licked her smaller tits and grinned.

Soon enough, the other two women joined in, shouting directions.

"Fuck her good, boys!"

"Now, let her taste your big, dirty cocks."

"Yes, lick it up, girl!"

"Now, Patrick, lick her little asshole clean. There's a good man..."

All five of them were soon writhing on the floor, sucking and penetrating one another. Nothing was forbidden them as they drank deep from the wells of one another's pleasure.

Together, Patrick and Jonathan

explored every orifice of the three women that night with their dicks. Each woman took it hard in the cunt, in the mouth, and in the ass. Often, two holes were filled at the same time, with the other women kissing and fondling one another.

At one point, Jonathan even shoved his substantial cock deep into Patrick's ass, which was something neither of them had done before. At first Patrick was frightened, but then he came to see that it felt good, having another man's warmth rubbing up against his prostate.

While Jonathan shafted the village leader, Crysteel and Donna came in from the sides down below and took turns sucking Patrick's dick. As they did this, they played with their own clits, listening to the instructions provided by Myra.

"Husband, work his sphincter raw. Pound that ass! Crysteel and Donna kiss each other and keep sucking that dick!"

Finally, Jonathan could withstand things no longer. He let out a great groan and came in Patrick's ass. His hot semen poured into his rectum and drooled out around Jonathan's still-pounding dick.

Feeling this hot invasion, Patrick came as well, shooting cum onto the faces of Crysteel and Donna both. "Ughh!" he cried.

Their lips and cheeks wet with cum, the succubus and the servant-girl resumed kissing each other, licking one another's faces clean and tasting Patrick's hot load.

As the moment wound down, Myra rubbed her pregnant belly with deep satisfaction. "Now that's how it's done!"

Patrick soon learned that it was the will of his new masters to offer them living space in his tower. In exchange, he was guaranteed some of the best damn sex he had ever imagined, whether he wanted it or not.

And as the days passed, he began to realize the power of the succubus and her ability to sexually bewitch men and women both. Yet, somehow, Jonathan was the true ringleader, and he had bigger plans than just sex. He wanted to use that sex to change the world.

How that would happen, exactly, remained to be seen.

4 A PERFECT FIT

The Leisure League of New Prime City had a new game out. It required full immersion and promised some of the best random anonymous sex of any game around. The players were dropped in the game at various stations in the virtual maze of a city called "Fuck Town." All the roads were convoluted connections between tower-like buildings of steel and glass. Other than that, it was like one gigantic Vegas hotel, wherein the players were expected to meet up with one another and have sex. Only, they would never have sex for too long, because each player was in a race to find that one other player whose genitals matched just right. The game was called "Perfect Fit," and Gordon Blomquist was one of its star players.

A skinny gamer with thick glasses in the real world, Blomquist always chose for his avatar, a tall and lanky albino male with a big, retrofitted dick. The dick was made of (if anything could truly be "made of" anything in the Virtual Land of Games) hard clear rubber, with clear balls filled with crystal blue semen. He had earned his avatar over years of victorious game play. Most of the other contestants were forced to assume their real-world identities.

When Blomquist first landed in the "Fuck Town" city maze, he found himself perched on a balcony overlooking the nighttime city skyline. Shuttlecraft flew by above the road down below. Turning away from the city, he looked to see what the balcony was attached to.

Right behind Blomquist was a huge bay window. Vanilla light spilled out through the glass, and he could hear muffled grunting as well. Peering in more closely, he saw a hefty man banging away atop a blonde bimbo.

With her mouth painted in cherry red lipstick, she calmly oohed and aahed, waiting for her temporary lover to realize their fit was not ideal.

Finally, noticing he was not getting much of a reaction, the hairy man pushed himself up off the woman and gathered his trousers. He then stormed out the room, looking for someone else to fuck.

That was when Blomquist tapped on the glass.

The blonde bimbo looked up and smiled lasciviously. She opened the sliding glass door and beckoned for her new suitor to enter.

Blomquist walked in and told the bitch to bend over.

She immediately planted her face in the couch. Reaching up and behind, she spread her ass cheeks so he could have a good look at her dripping pussy and black cherry of an asshole.

Wasting no time, Blomquist shoved his thick clear dick inside her hungry snatch. It felt good, the way she glued herself to his dick, but he doubted this was a perfect fit, because he was not all the way in, and already he could feel she was full.

When he started to pull out, she cried, "No! Let's try again. You have to fit!"

Either she was extremely desperate or she was a Bot designed to fool the unwary player. Blomquist grabbed her white ass cheeks and pushed her forward. She rolled off his dick and off the couch.

"But wait!" she cried again.

"Sorry, hon, you're not the one."

Having wandered out the bimbo's apartment, Blomquist found himself in a long, winding hallway. As he moved along, he could hear the sounds of sex coming from the rooms he passed by. He was such a skillful player: he could tell just by the sounds they were not perfect fits. He understood that a lot of players joined in these games just to have sex for the sake of sex, but he was always in it to win.

When he came to an elevator, he decided to use it. Inside, he saw a grown woman dressed like a sexy Japanese schoolgirl.

"What floor?" she politely asked.

"Ground."

With nails painted neon green to match her eyeliner, the woman pressed the button marked "1." She then proceeded to turn around, drop to her knees, and suck Blomquist's always-hard and ready dick.

It felt good, her lips wrapped around his unit, and he started to wonder if she might not be the one. It was highly unlikely that he should encounter his perfect fit so early in the game, but not unheard of. As she bobbed her head up and down along the length of his shaft, he let himself relax a bit, seeing where the sensations might lead him.

When she cupped his balls with her hands and nibbled lightly with her teeth on the head of his dick, he felt an unusual surge of pleasure. This girl really knew what she was doing. So, either she was the one or Blomquist needed to get away now!

But the elevator had not reached the ground floor yet, and Blomquist could not bear to pull his cock free of the hot sucking it was receiving.

Perhaps sensing Blomquist's concern, the Japanese woman pulled his dick out of her mouth with a loud popping sound and said, "You know, I think you and I are a match. I love the taste of your cock and want nothing more than to have it spill cum all up inside my aching vagina."

The elevator dinged, and the door slid open.

"Come with me," she said, pulling him into a wide-open room.

The room they entered was enormous. Glowing chandeliers hung from a vaulted ceiling, and the floor was filled with beds of all shapes and sizes. Round, spinning ones, four-posters, ones shaped like hearts, bunk beds... everything from single to king-size and beyond.

An orgy was going on, too.

There were couples and threesomes and even larger gatherings. They were doing all sorts of sex acts, from simple missionary to 69 to fisting and bukake. Most of the men and women here were just having fun. They did not expect to win the game and did not really care. But then Blomquist noticed one particular couple, in the middle of a giant waterbed, slowly fucking each other (in missionary position, no less!) as if nothing else in the world mattered beyond their conjoined cock and cunt.

Rapidly assessing the situation, Blomquist realized this was a couple very close to a winning orgasm.

Now, according to the rules of this particular game, the players were not allowed to physically interfere with each other. Therefore, violence was completely forbidden. This meant that Blomquist needed to make a gamble.

Pulling the Japanese schoolgirl by the hand, he dragged her right up next to the rippling waterbed. "Let me see your pussy!" he said, loud enough for the couple fucking in the waterbed to hear.

Using both her delightfully manicured hands, the Japanese woman flipped up her plaid skirt to show her pink panties. She then pressed her finger against the line of her cunt, causing her panties to indent and moisten. After this sexy little display, she bent way over and pulled her panties down past her ass and cunt, all the way to her ankles.

"Oh yeah! That's what I like to see." Blomquist could feel his cock already throbbing with anticipation. Gently but firmly pushing his schoolgirl down on her hands and knees, he squatted in a straddling position and rammed his cock home into her sweet, wet pussy.

"Ayyyyeee!" she cried out.

To his surprise, Blomquist's clear rubber dick sank down into her cunt and all the way up to his balls. It was a perfect fit, and they both knew it! Now they just had to come faster than this other couple on the bed.

"Don't stop!" shouted the nameless schoolgirl. "I want you to pump me all the way to Heaven!"

Blomquist looked past her upraised ass and made eye contact with the dark-haired man fucking the busty redhead in the waterbed. The man snarled, obviously distracted by all the noise Blomquist and his sexual partner were making. "Yes!" shouted Blomquist, as he slapped the schoolgirl's ass, as it bounced against his hips with every deep-dicked thrust.

The dark-haired man tried to reposition himself but found the waterbed too confining. He muttered a curse, and then the redhead looked angrily at Blomquist as well.

Blomquist smiled and waved, then gave the pussy on his dick a few good hard shots of his retrofitted rubber dick.

The Japanese woman dropped her

face to the floor and moaned in ecstasy.

Seeing that they were quickly losing their lead, the dark-haired man and his voluptuous sex partner clambered out of their bed. They had a hard time maneuvering across the swelling of the water in the waterbed, but finally they made it. They then took up a position just a few feet away from Blomquist and his partner. "I'm Kurt," said the dark-haired man.

"And I'm Natalia," said the redhead.

Blomquist laughed. "Sure. Whatever. Call me Gordon, 'cause I'm "Gordon-win" this game!"

Still being repeatedly penetrated by Blomquist, the Japanese schoolgirl stuttered her name between thrusts. "Ah! – I'm – ah! – Junko!"

Junko's name alone made Blomquist think of all the sexy Hentai images he used to masturbate to when he was younger. Dainty, cute Japanese doll-faced women, all with an aching desire to have their cunts stuffed with anything and everything, from dicks to tentacles. The images that flashed through his mind brought him just that much closer to orgasm.

The redhead nearby was beginning to moan. She squeezed her dark fat nipples as she rode her partner, who was now lying on the ground. She bounced up and down on his stiff cock, causing her substantial ass and breasts to jiggle in a very arousing way. She gave the man she was fucking a good show as well as a nice fit on his dick, sliding from tip to balls and back again, over and over.

Catching a glimpse of this action out of the corner of his eye, Blomquist realized they were about to come. Having the woman on top was a good idea, so Blomquist decided to do even better.

"C'mere, you!" Blomquist stopped plowing Junko from behind and held out his hand for her to grab. He then pulled her up, so they were both standing. Grabbing her pert little butt with both of his large and lanky hands, Blomquist hoisted Junko's petite body all the way up to his chest and then slid her down onto the tip of his dick.

"Oooooh!" she purred, as she was penetrated yet again. She reached up and held onto Blomquist's neck, ready for the ride of her life. "Fuck me, my big balled man! Fuck me hard!"

This was acrobatic sex, the kind few players would ever be able to manage, and Blomquist knew it. He felt his orgasm fast approaching and Junko's too, as she giggled and bounced on his hard knob.

Some of the other players even stopped their own sex play just to have a look at the show they were putting on. So they didn't miss anything, Blomquist pulled his hands apart against Junko's ass cheeks, splitting her wide so everyone could see her tight little asshole dancing above her repeatedly stuffed pussy. He knew the men on the side were getting a good look at her small tits as well.

The women players were especially taken with Blomquist tall authority and his unstoppable dick. A few of them even started playing with themselves, preferring to masturbate to Blomquist than be fucked by their own substandard partners.

It was then that Junko made the perfect move. Taking control, she lifted herself up almost completely off Blomquist's dick and then dropped herself back down on his cock harder than he could ever hope to thrust. The sexual energy of that impact, when their perfectly matched cock and cunt slammed against each other, one inside the other, sent ripples of ecstasy coursing through both their bodies.

Neither Blomquist nor Junko was thinking anything at all. They did not worry about their competitors; they did not need to win the game (which they were winning, by the way). All they cared about was the thunderous climax building at the base of Blomquist's balls to shoot like a rocket up into Junko's welcoming red cunt. The sensation was deep and mighty. Blomquist felt like his dick was turning itself inside out with pleasure.

The orgasm shattered every record the game had ever known. Junko screamed in wild release as she was split apart by Blomquist's rubber dick now shooting streaming blue cum all up inside her. She cried out, tears streaming past her painted eyelids, and clung to his neck, hanging there with sweet exhaustion.

As they came down from their high, Blomquist and little Junko – still perched on the tip of his flawless dick –

both heard the sound of applause. The other gamers were actually clapping, having never seen a game come to such a marvelous close.

They were a perfect fit, indeed!

5 THE MISSING DILDO

The week had been difficult for Keith Peters, a detective in private practice in the big city of Los Angeles. The week started with the assignment on the Rutherford case. It seemed Mrs. Rutherford did not take a liking to her husband's extramarital dalliances and was bound and determined to catch him at it. So she wanted photographic proof that would stand up in court.

Only, the strange thing was that every time Peters got a tip regarding a potential meet-up between Mr. Rutherford and one of his little whores, the tip proved to be a bust. He stood outside fashionable restaurants, trolled throughout the hilly terrain of Griffith Park, and otherwise made a low-key fool of himself trying to squeeze juice from his leads.

Also, by the second day on the case, Peters began receiving anonymous gifts in the mail. They were addressed to him in nondescript handwriting printed in ballpoint on brown paper wrapping, always neatly taped shut around a thin white cardboard box. The box would be stuffed with clippings from porn magazines. The gift, whatever it might happen to be, was always tucked inside.

The first gift was a pair of handcuffs lined in pink silk; the second, a pair of champagne glasses; the third, a bottle of bubbly; and the fourth, a dildo.

This last one was about 8 inches long from end to end, all smooth white plastic except for the removable end, also white, but with a ribbon of gold encircling the nub. When Peters had twisted the end of the dildo, he had expected to find a place for batteries inside, as it was probably a vibrator. But when he opened this particular item, he discovered it contained the assembly of a working ink pen. So it was a dildo rather than a vibrator – a dildo one could write with.

Odd.

Peters sat at his wooden desk in his back office, with the light of the setting sun coming through his window. He was scratching his head, trying to figure out how all these things might possibly be connected. The items were lined on his desk, so he could look at them all at once.

Beatrice, his secretary, was in the front room trying to reassemble the torn-up pieces of porn magazine just in case a clue might be hidden there. He imagined what her reaction might be, unfolding and flattening colorful images of various genitals, all in compromising positions. He smiled, thinking of her touching herself as she looked at the pictures.

She was a fine piece of flesh, his secretary was – a fine piece of sexy flesh he was professionally bound never to tap. Maybe. But if she ever came on to him in the right way, he would certainly have a very difficult time saying no. After all, how does one say no to an hourglass figure comprised of big succulent tits and a beautifully inverted heart of an ass?

As if she sensed him thinking about her, Beatrice click-clacked her high heels into Peters' office and reported on her progress. "The cuttings are all too random, Mr. Peters. I can't piece much of anything together, so I think the only message in the cuttings is the fact they were taken from porn magazines." She gave a light cough. "Dirty, dirty porn magazines, I might add."

"Do they offend you, Bee?"

"Only because I know I could do much better." She dropped two file folders on Peters' desk.

"What are these?"

"The latest from Mrs. Rutherford." She started to saunter back into the front office, but then stopped to turn back around. She eyed the items on his desk, the dildo in particular. "You want me to put these things away for the night, or do you need them out here cluttering the desk after you leave?"

"Okay. Fine. Yes, please. Put them in that box over there and keep them under your desk, with the porn clippings." Peters leaned back in his plush office chair, stretching.

The secretary moved to the side of the room and bent down to pick up the box. Bending at the hips, rather than the knees, she afforded Peters a delightful view of her red silk panties underneath her black satin miniskirt. Her panties barely covered her plump little cunt, and he felt like he had just seen heaven.

When she stood up and turned back around, she noticed how Peters was looking at her. "Ahem," she said. "I think maybe it's time to call it a night." As she picked up the items on the desk and placed them in the box, the red fingernail polish she wore flashed brightly. It was the same red as the red of her panties, hugging her twat.

"Yes. I'll be out in a second." Peters did not want to get up right away, as he had a hard-on the size of a downtown skyscraper pressing against his pants.

Beatrice click-clacked out of the room, carrying the box at her side and giving Peters a parting shot of her smooth round ass.

Tomorrow would be another day.

When Peters arrived at his office the next morning, he discovered Beatrice had not yet arrived, which was unusual. He raised the blinds and organized his desk before pulling the box of mysterious gifts out from under her desk to have a look at those items one more time.

Sitting down, he pulled out of the open box the bottle of champagne first, then one of the glasses. He carefully stood these up together on the right side of his desk. Reaching in again, pushing aside the bits of torn porn mags, he grabbed hold of the second glass and the handcuffs. The dildo, however, was nowhere to be found.

Concerned, he picked up the phone and dialed Bee's home number. All he got was her answering machine, and he decided not to leave a message.

Then, he heard the toilet flush. Behind the closed bathroom door in his office, someone was flushing the toilet. He thought it might be Bee, but then the office should have been open when he arrived.

Carefully pulling his pistol out of his

shoulder holster, Peters crept up to the bathroom door. He listened carefully, trying to ascertain who might be on the other side and what they were doing.

He heard a satisfied sigh, then the sound of someone washing his or her hands in the sink. After a moment, the water was turned off and paper towels were pulled from the dispenser. Finally, he heard what sounded like a low, feminine moan, followed by the snap of fabric against skin.

Peters drew back, not knowing what to think.

Finally, the door opened.

Peters aimed his gun.

Beatrice screamed. "Aaaaah!"

"Christ, woman, what are you doing?"

"Taking a shit," she stated matter-of-factly.

"Yes, but you could have given me a sign you were here."

"I didn't hear you come in!"

"Well, the door was locked." Peters slid his pistol back in its holster. "And one of those gifts is missing."

"Oh, really?" Beatrice looked innocently about the room. "Which one?"

"The... dildo." Peters noticed Beatrice was standing up straighter than usual. "You wouldn't have any idea where it might be, would you?"

"No. Did you look around the office?"

"Not yet. Why don't you help me?"

"Okay."

They both pretended to look about the office. Beatrice's heart did not really seem too invested in the search, and Peters was too busy watching her to look effectively himself. He noticed that she seemed to be walking a bit more carefully than normal, too.

"Beatrice."

"Yes?" Dressed in a low-cut blue sundress today, the secretary played with the gold chain hanging between her melon-sized tits.

"It seems to me you're hiding something."

"What do you mean, Mr. Peters?"

"I mean that you are acting suspiciously." He pulled his office chair in front of his desk next to Beatrice and took a seat. "Now. You are going to participate in the little investigation we're about to perform, or you'll be out on the street with your beautiful ass in a sling."

"Why, Mr. Peters. I had no idea you admired my ass."

"We'll get to that. But first, I need you to take off your shoes."

Slowly bending over so her tits hung down and swayed before her like plump ripe fruit, Beatrice carefully undid and stepped out of her black high heels, which matched her dark ponytail. Now standing with fishnet stocking feet on the floor, Beatrice awaited further orders.

"The sundress, now. Take it off."

"Why, Mr. Peters. This is highly inappropriate."

"Are you going to tell me where the dildo is?"

"No."

"Then this investigation will continue!"

Flashing Peters a provocative look of frustration, Beatrice pulled the sundress up over and off her goddess-like figure. She had on white lace panties and bra, perfectly matched. Their color was a lovely contrast against her tan skin, especially her taut tummy, which looked good enough to eat from. Feeling a pinch, she lifted one of her tits up a bit, adjusting the way it rode in the bra. "Well, Mr. Peters? The dildo is not in my bra, as you can plainly see."

"I wouldn't be so sure of that. Take it off."

"But...."

Peters opened his vest, revealing the pistol still in its holster.

Beatrice quickly unbuttoned her bra and let it fall to the ground. Her tits sank down to their natural but still perky resting place, the nipples large and round. "Do you need to check inside by tits, Mr. Peters?"

"Yes. I think I will." The private detective stood up from his chair and grabbed Beatrice by her slender shoulders. Gorgeous in nothing but her white panties and fishnet stockings, she looked so good to Peters that he could not help himself. Hungry now, he dipped his head down to her left tit and began sucking her hardening nipple there.

Beatrice gave a little cry of pleasure and dropped to her knees. Attacking his trousers with her hands, she undressed Peters just enough to free his bulging cock. She then sank it in her mouth, swallowing it all down with repetitive slurps.

With his hands on the back of her head, Peters fucked her beautiful skull until she gagged and drooled. "I can see the dildo is not in your mouth, either. But still, I must search your throat as well."

Eager to please her handsome employer, Beatrice widened her throat, letting his dick perform a thorough inspection of her primary facial orifice. "God, that feels good!" She shouted when he pulled out, saliva dripped past her chin.

"Well, if it isn't in your mouth...." Peters bent down over Beatrice's beautiful body to grab her panties and rip them firmly off her bulbous ass. Looking over, he caught a glimpse of white and gold. "A-ha!"

"What, Mr. Peters?"

"The dildo is here... in..."

"Where?"

"Your anus!"

Beatrice blinked her big innocent eyes. "Oh, you mean this thing?" She reached behind herself and pulled out all eight inches of the mysterious dildo. "Is this what you were looking for?"

"Let me see it."

She handed it to him.

He then waved it under her nose before pressing it softly into her mouth.

She licked at it, tasting her ass juice and smiled. "Oh, baby. Could you make your dick taste this good?"

Peters said nothing more, cutting to the chase. He tossed the dildo to the floor, not interested in ever unraveling its mystery... at least not before he unraveled the mystery of Beatrice's asshole on his cock. He lifted her up and pushed her onto the desk.

With her hands around Peters' neck, Beatrice sat on her lower back. Her legs wrapped around his hips and her tight little asshole, done with the dildo, she was more than ready to receive his thrusting cock.

Shoving his manhood up the brown hole in the middle of her rear, Peters marveled at the way her tits jiggled. He grabbed her ass cheeks and squeezed them, feeling her soft flesh almost bruise in his hands.

He had left her cunt out of the equation, but – based on her cries of ecstasy – she did not resent him for it. In fact, she seemed to enjoy the good hard ass fucking more than most women would appreciate it in their twats.

When he came, it was inside her asshole. He pumped three or four times, leaving his hot load up her rectum, and then withdrew to sit back down in his chair.

He may have had other business to tend to, but for now it was more than enough just to watch her push his cum out of her asshole with a sexy audible flutter into her receiving hand... which she then licked clean like every good girl should.

6 NAKED NURSE

Sir Goodwin had led the charge in many a battle, but never before had he fallen so quickly. He remembered running across the drawbridge, his metal armor clanking in its leather supports, with his five best men behind him. His first opponent was a childish sword bearer, of whom Goodwin made a quick dispatch. Then a taller man shielded in chain mail stood before our valiant hero with mace in hand.

Goodwin thrust sharply with his long sword, making room for his companions to pass.

The mace-wielding fighter blocked Goodwin's long sword with his small shield. He then moved in to attack. At least, that is what he started to do. But then, he stepped back a bit, making room for something Goodwin could not see.

Goodwin paused, unsure of what to make of things.

It was then that an enemy with a war hammer struck a blow against Goodwin's helm from behind.

After that, everything had gone black.

Until the moment, Goodwin found himself in now, with his world one of great pain. His head ached, and he could hear the sharp but faint sound of pouring water.

"Uhh..." He propped open one eye, only to see a blur of red and white against a dark background. The image seemed to flicker, as if it were a candle.

"He's awake now. Set the pitcher down and leave us be, servant." The voice was that of a womanly angel, so pure of pitch it was.

"Yes, nurse," answered a man of slurred speech.

Goodwin heard the man stepped away. He then noticed he could not feel the weight of his armor, although he did seem to be covered, perhaps, by a blanket. Again, his head throbbed with great discomfort, and he closed his eyes. At least he was in a comfortable bed.

"Be still, my valiant knight. I must wash your wound."

Delicate yet competent hands tilted Goodwin's head to the side. He heard the pitcher being dipped into a trough and then felt the cool wash of water against the back of his head.

"He got me good, didn't he?"

"Indeed, but you are in good hands now, Sir Knight." The nurse carefully cleaned his wound. "You took a blow to the head, but I believe you will recover quickly... with the proper attention."

"What do I need, my lady?"

"Oh, I think something having to do with my body... and yours. Something, how shall we say, intimate?"

Goodwin pulled his attention away from his aching cranium to focus on the rest of his body. He did indeed seem fine. In fact, he noticed he even had a bit of an erection, no doubt due to the mellifluous voice of the nurse and her suggestive words.

"My lord," said the nurse, "you appear to be healing faster than anticipated."

Goodwin—not knowing what to expect—was pleasantly surprised when the nurse's hand pressed against his blanketed hard-on. "Ahh... nurse... I..."

"Hush, Sir Knight. I think it wise to examine you further."

Fighting to open his eyes once more, Goodwin managed to see things more clearly.

They were in a small, cave-like room. The only light came from a pair of small torches hung from opposite walls. The nurse, who was now pulling away Goodwin's blanket, was a stunning brunette, wearing a red shawl over a white blouse. Even though she was fully clothed, he could see she was blessed with substantial breasts. He could only imagine her ass was just as nicely rounded.

"Excellent," she said. "Although you do not appear to have been injured down here, I think it best we examine things thoroughly." With that having been said, the nurse then proceeded to fondle her patient's quickly growing cock until it stood at full attention. "This is a lovely lance you have here, My Lord."

"My lady, will not someone be coming soon?"

"Oh no, Sir Knight. Not before we do." She smiled seductively and began to actively stroke his dick.

Goodwin felt a tingling in his balls. She was right, he thought, he would come indeed.

The nurse bent down and kissed the tip of his dick. Then, using a swirling motion with her tongue, she bathed his cock in spittle, slick and warm. Slowly now, she took the length of him in her mouth and to the back of her throat, catching for a moment with the slightest of gag reflexes but then taking him all the way down. "Mmm..." She moaned and sped up her movements, pulling his dick out past her lips and back in again as far as it could go.

Goodwin could feel his balls tighten and his dick begin to drip in the nurse's mouth.

"Ahh... you taste wonderful, Sir Knight." She ran her fingers across her lips and stood up next to the bed. "I think it terribly unfair that you should be the only one without clothes at this particular moment in time." Smiling, the nurse then proceeded to remove her shawl and to pull her blouse up over her voluptuous body. Her nipples stood out like dark sentinels on ivory hills, while her carefully shaven wrinkles hung in loose folds between her smooth legs.

Goodwin felt his dick grow even harder at the sight of this beautiful naked nurse.

"Do you think you might sit up for me, my good man?"

Cautious not to hurt himself, Goodwin pushed himself up into a sitting position. He felt a little dizzy, but the sensation quickly subsided. Without even asking, he reached out with his hand to press against the nurse's cunt.

"Ooh! My Lord! Such strong hands for such a tender subject!"

Goodwin leaned down and parted her pussy lips, revealing the pink between. He then rubbed her swelling clit with his thumb.

"Aah! It feels so good. I do believe

you will recover just fine. But we still need to see how that dick of yours works..." The nurse stepped to the side and slapped her own ass invitingly, then bent down, placing both hands on the side of the bed.

Standing now, the injured knight followed his erection to its proper destination, sliding it firmly inside the hole that was the nurse's now-blossoming flower of desire.

Bending down even further, to reveal more fully her plump bottom, the nurse sighed with the pleasure of each languid thrust. It was a slow fucking, one of great feeling and thorough penetration.

"Do you think me well, My Lady?"

"I do indeed, good Sir Knight. Only, I find myself in need of a good hard fuck, now." She dropped her face on the bed and reached up and behind to spread her ass cheeks as wide as they would go. "Care to deliver?"

Goodwin was awestruck by what he saw. There was her cunt, still gaping from the absence of his sizable dick, and above it was the cleanest, most perfect pucker of an asshole he had ever seen. Beginning to salivate, he dropped to his knees and buried his face between her ass cheeks. He stuck his tongue out and curled it around her clit, before dragging his taste buds up her slit all the way to her asshole. Tongue-fucking her brown hole, he gripped her ass cheeks with both hands.

"Ooh! This was not what I expected, but I like it just the same!" The nurse purred softly. "You're not going to put that sizable cock of yours up my ass, are you?"

Goodwin laughed, as the nurse wiggled her butt from side to side.

Not wanting to injure that lovely asshole of hers, Goodwin stood once more and reinserted himself into her moist twat. He then gave her the good hard fucking she had asked for earlier, pulling her hips up against his own so as to bury his dick inside as deep as it could go.

The nurse began to tremble from the slick friction of their fucking. "Every hole is yours, Sir Knight! Every hole!" Bouncing her butt cheeks back and forth along his shuttling shaft, she cried out for more.

Grabbing the pitcher of water,

Goodwin poured it over her ass and slapped her wet skin. He then turned her round, until she was upside down, looking up between her legs, with her ass raised upward and exposed for the deepest of penetration.

"Sir Knight!"

Smacking his nurse's ass one more time, Goodwin squatted over her and pressed his dick down into her black cherry of an asshole. His cock filled her rectum, causing her gaping pussy to flex out for room. As he drove his cock in and out of her ass, he could feel his orgasm coming on strong, so he pulled out and took a few deep breaths.

As he struggled to regain control, he looked down to see her asshole, now gaping as well, flexing open and closed in contracting circles.

Her soothing turn-on of a voice sounded out over the sputtering of the torches. "Well, your cock has passed three tests so far: that of the mouth, that of the pussy, and that of the ass. But there is one test remaining, before I can give you a clean bill of health."

"And what is that, my dear?" asked Goodwin as he shook his dick, limbering it up for more action.

"A taste test, of course..." The nurse bit her lip ever so coyly.

"I thought you already said I tasted good." Goodwin grinned.

"I did indeed, Sir Knight, but there is much more—sticky and gooey—to taste." She licked her lips.

Seeing her point, the knight raised his nurse up off the ground and set her gently on the bed, with her head hanging backward over the edge.

"Yes," she said, "this will be an excellent position from which I may receive your sample of goodly sperm, indeed." Opening her mouth, she playfully stuck out her tongue and said, "Aahhh!"

"Let's see how we do." Goodwin then shoved his dick into her mouth, his balls hitting her nose, and watched her throat expand and contract with the rhythm of his thrusts. In the same rhythm, her ample breasts spilled out to the side and shook back and forth.

The sound of the throat fuck was sloppy and slick. The nurse gagged a number of times. Spit drooled past her nose and down her forehead.

Grabbing her delicious tits with his fists, Goodwin pulled out to let her breath.

She gasped for air with choking moans of delight.

He then changed his angle a bit so he could really slam her throat hard.

It was only a matter of time before the orgasm formed at the base of his sacrum. It grew and grew there, swelling up into his balls until they were full to bursting. Then, with one particularly forceful thrust, the orgasm raced up the shaft of his cock to explode in a shower of semen. Cumming deep in her throat, Goodwin slowly withdrew.

Coughing a bit and smiling, the nurse flipped up onto her knees on the bed. She spit up in her hand and breathed in deeply through her nose the smell of the mixture of semen and saliva that was pooled in her palm. Wiping this sexy wet over her lips, she licked all around the outside of her mouth, tasting Goodwin's flavor.

"Well?" asked Goodwin, wondering when he would have the opportunity to do this again.

"Absolutely delicious, My Lord." After swallowing down what was left of Goodwin's hot load, the nurse rolled back and propped up her pussy. "Kiss me now, Sir Knight. I do believe you are healed!"

Bending down ever so slowly, Goodwin touched his lips to the nurse's sweet and fragrant flower of a pussy one last time. She was warm there from being fucked so well, and when he pulled away, he knew he had been taken care of by the best of them.

Whatever battles lay ahead, he was certain that if this woman was waiting in the wings to nurse him back to health, he could take on anything.

7 DIRTY DRAWINGS

Ever since the buxom beauty Beth-Anne – one of the ladies of the court – had snubbed his advances, the wizard Garrondello had begun thinking a lot more seriously about the fairies that lived in nearby Fairy Hill. From his tower at night, he could see the hill and all the lovely commotion there. From a distance, it looked like dancing lights, when the naked glowing bodies of the fairies would move about to the rhythm of inaudible music; but what Garrondello really liked to do was to sneak a peek at the Fairy Hill Scribe.

The scribe of Fairy Hill, named Orestia, often sat outside the hill all by herself, writing in her little fairy book, the chronicles of fairy affairs, or maps of their adventurous exploits. She glowed green and was the loveliest to the magically aided eyes of Garrondello. When she brushed her long fine hair over her feminine shoulders, Garrondello was watching. When she sucked on the end of her pen between her plump little lips, Garrondello was watching. When she bent over to pick a book up off the ground, Garrondello was watching for sure because that was when her shaved pussy poked out between her legs under her scrumptious derrière.

For a time, Garrondello drew pictures of Orestia in all kinds of revealing positions, taking magical snapshots of her tits and ass whenever she moved just right. These pictures were a serious turn-on for the wizard, who would often masturbate to them. Sadly, this was all he could reasonably hope to do, he being over five feet tall and Orestia no more than one single foot in height.

One night, he prayed to the Gods of Magic for them to show him a way to truly make love to the gorgeous winged fairy that was the object of his desires. Stroking one out in the name of his wish, Garrondello closed his eyes and went to sleep.

In his dream, Garrondello saw a beautiful ink pen and a scroll. Next to these items, Orestia fluttered in the air. She landed on the table. The pen then moved of its own accord and inscribed on the parchment a sketch of Garrondello. Suddenly, Garrondello himself stepped off of the paper to find he was standing on the wooden table with Orestia. They were finally of the same size. She was naked and beautiful. She smiled, and he quickly removed his clothing. She came closer, her hand stroked his cock, and then... the dream ended!

"Curses!" muttered Garrondello as he woke up from his dream. He turned over in his cot and thought a moment. "What if?"

He jumped to his feet and wildly searched about his wizardly laboratory. He had seen that scroll and ink pen before! They were somewhere in this very lab! But where?

The wizard grabbed one of the sketches of Orestia to calm his thoughts. There she was, leaning over a large mushroom with her pert tits hanging there like fresh fruit. Think, Garrondello! Where is the pen and paper?

He remembered!

Racing to the side of the room, he cracked open an old iron chest. The objects he sought were inside!

Garrondello spent the day working on his spell, finding the proper ingredients and composing the words. Then, as the sun set, he cast his spell:

May this pen be her pen
The pen of Orestia, the Scribe
And with it, may she draw for herself
Images of us having sex
Increasing her desire until
She wishes me through the page!
Before the Gods of Magic
I have now set the stage!

His incantation was perfect, and Garrondello knew it. Now he had only to test things out tonight!

Orestia was sitting on her usual mushroom stool, looking up at the stars and composing in her book. What she did not know though was what she was about to draw once she turned the page! She felt a tugging at her pen. Looking down, she discovered that her hand was already drawing something. She drew her own pretty face and shining green hair. She looked at the page with wide eyes as she drew things not of her own accord.

What she drew next was a great big fat and veined cock. As she sketched this extraordinary member, she could not help but blush and think how much she would love to see one like that for real. With her other hand, she pinched a nipple, making sure she was not dreaming, and then she began to rub her clit. Her reddening pussy lips got all swollen as she masturbated to the drawing of this mysterious hunk of man-flesh.

"Oh!" she cried, pressing her pussy-moistened hand up against her mouth. Then she tasted herself there and moaned.

All a-fluster, Orestia turned the page once more and began a new sketch. It was again of her face, only this time her mouth was open wide and her tongue stuck out to lick the head of that monstrously desirable cock.

"Oh!" she cried again, thinking how wonderful it would be to taste that dick.

She knew what she wanted to draw next, and she did. In her picture, she swallowed that dick all the way down the back of her throat. She even managed to fit those bulging balls into her mouth as well. It was such a marvelous picture.

"I want more," she purred.

Next she drew pictures of herself, playing with her pussy and showing it off to this man who promised to fuck her into endless ecstasy. She stretched her lips open with her hands, opening the hole there and inviting his tongue to lick her there.

More of his body began to appear in the pictures. After his cock, next was his tongue, then his hands, squeezing and spreading her round little ass cheeks wide, then his hips and buttocks as he fucked her hard. Pretty soon, she had a good idea what this man looked like.

He was not the handsomest fellow in the world. He was even a little old, and a little skinny, but his cock was something to die for. Seriously, it was big and thick and seemed to fit into her cunt just right!

Looking through all the drawings she had made of herself and this man having sex, Orestia played with her pussy one last time. Flicking her clit with one of her index fingers, she used the fingers on her other hand to fuck herself. She moaned in concert with the moist sound of her fingers banging and came – not just once but three times. That last climax caused her to squirt all over her mushroom throne.

Exhausted, she whispered to the heavens, "Ye Gods, I wish he were real and here to fuck me raw!"

And her wish was granted.

Just like magic – because that was what it was – Garrondello stepped out of Orestia's book of drawings. Bigger than the drawings themselves, but much smaller than life, Garrondello was a perfect match for the green Fairy Orestia. Finally, the wizard could do more than just masturbate to simple images, however lovely they might be. Now he could taste the sweet nectar of this otherworldly forest creature with his own lips and tongue!

When the fairy first saw Garrondello, she gasped with delight and fell off her mushroom seat. Landing on all fours, she afforded the wizard a spectacular view of her rear, already glistening with wet because she had been playing with herself for so long. "My Lord!" she cried, looking over her shoulder to turn around. "Are you real? May I only bring you as much pleasure as your images have brought to me!"

Garrondello, himself as naked as the fairy, cupped his balls and stroked his cock. It engorged itself as he looked upon Orestia's small but well-rounded tits. "I am indeed real, my lovely! Come, approach me, and tell me how you would please me most."

Smiling wide, Orestia crawled toward the wizard and sat at his feet. Then, almost shyly, she looked up at his hardening cock. "First, I would suck this beautiful dick of yours just as long and hard as you would like." She then stood up on her knees, bringing her beautiful face level with the very dick of which she spoke. She licked it once, very lightly, just at its tip. She giggled playfully and withdrew a bit.

Garrondello, having longed for such a great while for this very moment, put his hands in her hair and guided her mouth back where it belonged. Once she opened her mouth, he then pulled her to him, thrusting the entire great length of his flesh into her mouth and up against the back of her throat.

She choked, but did not resist. Even though it was almost too much for her, his cock was just where she wanted it right now. Relaxing, she let the head of his cock slide down her throat. Then she looked up into the wizard's eyes, begging him to fuck her deeper.

He obliged, pulling back his cock only to thrust it even deeper a second time... and a third... and more... all in a fierce rhythm that gave Orestia just the slightest chance to breathe briefly, in wet gasps, as her spit poured out of her mouth over his cock and down her chest.

"Ahhhhhhhh!" she finally cried out, able to breathe freely once more. "I love the taste of it! Please, feed me more!"

The wizard lay down on the grass, next to the mushroom, his cock pointing to the sky. "Certainly my dear. Dinner is served."

The petite fairy then hopped on top of her magical lover, her mouth again on his cock and her swelling pussy just above his head so he could watch her play with herself while she sucked his dick. She let out muffled moans as she stuffed his cock deep down her throat, and she was so wet that her pussy juices actually dribbled on Garrondello's chin.

Getting a good whiff of her horny scent, the wizard raised his mouth and pressed it up against her quivering cunt. He lapped at her there like a thirsty mongrel, enjoying the slick texture on his lips and against his tongue.

She began to shake. Raising her head up from her work, Orestia ground back down on the wizard's face, writhing in sweet orgasm. She let out a stuttering yelp, "Uh – uh – ahhh!" Then she fell to the side and rolled on her back. She felt like a lifeless doll, overwhelmed with pleasure.

It was then that Garrondello took her

legs in his arms and pressed them together up over her chest.

She looked past her legs with an expression of helpless arousal. "Oh, yes." Grabbing her ankles with her hands, she leaned back a bit, raising her ass off the ground and spreading her legs wide. She opened herself completely.

The wizard knew exactly what to do next. Holding his throbbing cock with one hand, he guided it up against her wetness. Then he moved it around, teasing her hungry vagina and getting his cock well lubricated. When she was finally about to explode with longing, he took the head of his cock and pressed it against her pussy lips. In one long, slow motion, he slid his cock all the way in, up to his balls. He filled her completely.

"Oh! Tease me no more!" she cried. "Fuck me like a lion!"

At her command, Garrondello pulled back until the head of his cock started to flash outside her pussy lips, and then he plunged right back in, fast and hard. Again and again, with great speed, he almost emptied her completely before filling her up with all the man-meat she could take.

"Yes! Fuck me, my lord! Fuck me!"

Garrondello held himself above her, fucking her like a stallion, waiting for the moment of his own release. He watched as her small tits bounced with every thrust and felt the way her pussy grabbed his cock. He heard the sound of moist air flutter past her pussy lips and he smiled.

"Oh! Please, don't stop! Fuck me harder!"

The wizard then dove in deep, burying his cock all the way to its balled hilt. He stopped there, holding it in and pressing her insides. Then he started to grind round and round.

She lost all control, squirting fluid all around his dick.

He pumped deep in quick short thrusts until he could feel his own orgasm coming on like a thunderstorm. Then, quickly, he pulled out and stroked his cock above her perfect belly. His cum shot out in white spurts and pooled in her navel. He then rubbed what was left of his erection up inside her pussy before he pulled out one final time and collapsed to the ground.

His eyes began to close, but before they did, he was granted one last parting gift. He got to see Orestia wipe the cum in her navel up with her fingers and lick it all away.

"Uhmmm...."

8 THE RING OF SEXUAL WISHES

Robert Higgins had been eighteen and horny for five months now, yet he was still a virgin. Even though he made bread for the village every day, even though he was far from ugly, and even though his father owned the bread shop, he still was not getting laid. When he really thought about it, the reason was obvious. It was because he kept to himself, never daring to strike up a conversation with any of the women of the village.

He would see beautiful women come into the store to purchase bread for their families, and all he could do was wish he had the courage to talk to them. But talking was not all he wanted. He wanted to see the women he talked to naked. He wanted them to spread their legs and invite him inside. He wanted them to suck his cock with their pretty mouths so he could watch their heavy breasts jiggle while they sucked. He wanted sex, plain and simple.

But all he ever did was talk the business of bread in the most boring ways imaginable. He knew he had to change, but he just did not know how to go about it. Having hardly any friends of even the male variety, he had nowhere to turn for advice. He had heard, however, that saying a prayer to the Fairy Queen of the Golden Forest might prove beneficial. So every night before he went to bed, he asked the Fairy Queen to show him how to get laid.

Not even that seemed to work, however.

Until...

A stranger entered the bread shop, a beautiful stranger; the woman must have traveled far, as Robert could not recall ever seeing anyone quite like her before. She had lovely brown hair held down with a crown of flowers and electric gray eyes. The dress she wore was like something a princess might don before heading out into the fields to pick daisies, formfitting green lace that accentuated her ample bosom and otherwise slender figure. She even wore a miniature, fully blossomed red rose as a ring on her right index finger.

"Good morning, bread maker." Her voice was soothing to Robert's ears. "My name is Welzanne, and I have come to this fine establishment to acquire sweetbread for myself." She looked about the wooden store, eyeing the simple breads on display.

"We don't have much call for sweetbread," said Robert.

"Then I suggest you make some up." Something in her stare was both demanding and difficult to ignore.

"Let me see what I have in back." Robert hurried to the storage room and found one last loaf of sweetbread, which he brought out to give to the lovely Welzanne. "Here you are!"

Welzanne broke off a piece of the bread with her delicate fingers and took a taste. "Oh, no. This will not do. It needs to be much sweeter... with cinnamon in it, at least." She set the piece of bread she had nibbled down on the counter, next to the broken loaf. "Make another. I will be back this same time tomorrow morning. If your offering pleases me, I shall reward you well." She then blew Robert a kiss, before turning around to leave the shop.

Robert spent the day filling orders for bread for a number of the village's more beautiful women. There was Adele, the whimsical redhead who always wore her hair in pigtails and liked to talk about how boring she thought her husband was. There was Marian, the vivacious blonde who was being courted by at least seven men from the village. And there was Jillian, the sultry full-figured brunette who took every opportunity to show off her physical assets. At least, that's what Robert had heard through the grapevine, as he had never had the courage to talk much to any of these lovelies.

Today was a little different, though. He did step out of his comfort zone enough to ask each of them what they liked in sweetbreads, and if they had any suggestions on how to make them better.

They each offered their advice, and as they did so, seemed to take second notice of Robert, the man behind the counter at the bread shop, whom they had always ignored before.

When it was time to close up shop, Robert stayed behind to work on creating a couple of loaves of sweetbread. He wanted them to be just perfect, so that the lovely Welzanne would reward him... hopefully with a hand job, at least! With sexy thoughts running through his horny head, Robert spent the evening at work and by the morning he would have his product ready for Welzanne's approval.

When Welzanne entered the bread shop the next morning, she was dressed exactly the same as she was the day before, although everything about her looked fresh – especially her supple tits. "Okay. Let's try this again. Have you any sweetbread?"

Robert immediately offered up the two loaves of bread he had slaved over the day before.

"Ah, two loaves. Such a perfect number." As she reached for the loaves in front of her, Welzanne pressed her arms together, causing her breasts to pop up and out. It was her not-so-subtle way of pointing out the perfection of the number two, especially when it came to loaves.

She then took a piece from the loaf on the right and gave it a taste. "Mmm! Delicious, Robert! It makes my mouth water..."

Robert blushed.

Welzanne laughed. "Oh, Robert. Your mind never wanders far, does it?"

"Far from what?"

"Why, from sex, my dear boy."

Robert blushed all the more.

"Here. I promised you a reward, and a reward you shall have. Only, don't waste it!" She then removed from her finger the rose ring and carefully handed it over to the bread maker. "This flower will not wilt until it has granted three wishes – three wishes that never ask anyone to do anything they do not already wish to do. Use them wisely!"

Welzanne then sprouted fairy wings

and flew out the door!

Robert was shocked and amazed, and now he had a magic ring of wishes at his disposal...

Before anyone else came into the shop, Robert made his first wish. "I wish Adele would come in here and want to have sex with me!"

As soon as Robert had spoken his wish, Adele came walking through the door. "Ohhh!" she said dramatically, "I want something different today. Bread maker, do you have anything sweet to put in my mouth?"

"Uh – I have these two loaves of sweetbread I just made last night." He pointed to the loaves left behind by Welzanne.

"Hmm. Let me try some." Smacking her ruby lips a couple of times, she said, "Well, it is tasty, but I think my mouth is hungry for something more..." She raised herself up onto the counter so she could look down at Robert's pants. "Don't you have something else down there?"

Robert blushed. "I, uh..."

Then Adele simply reached down between his legs and gave a tug. "Yes, this is what I want!" She climbed completely over the counter and dropped down behind it, pulling Robert's pants open to unfold his growing hard-on. "Mmm. This will do quite nicely."

She licked his dick until it grew to full size and then began bobbing her head along the length of his shaft, stroking him with her tongue.

"Oh!" Robert moaned. "That feels so good."

Just then, Marian entered the shop.

When Robert saw this second beautiful woman, all the while feeling the tremendous pleasure of Adele giving him head behind the counter, he tried to act normal. "Hello, Marian. Ah! – uh, what can I do for you today?"

"Just the usual. Say, how did that sweetbread turn out?"

"Better than I could have imagined!"

Adele chose that moment to swallow Robert's cock as deep as it would go. Then she lightly bit down with her teeth as she pulled his cock back all the way out of her mouth.

"Is this the bread on the table?"

"Yes!" Robert could barely concentrate; Adele was giving him such good head. "Try some."

"Why, thank you." Marian tore off a piece of the bread and ate it. Then she noticed how oddly Robert was standing. "Are you – uh..." She looked down and saw Adele's red pigtails bouncing in front of Robert's waist. "I – why, I never!" She looked angry now, and started to turn around, no doubt to leave the shop.

Robert immediately made another wish: "I wish Marian would not leave, but join in, instead!"

Suddenly, Marian stopped her turning and looked back at Robert with lustful eyes. "Ah!" She saw the ring on his finger. "You know, it isn't fair to wish me into having sex with you. Or, well, it wouldn't be if I didn't think you were cute." She lifted up her dress to show off her pussy. "You can have this, Robert, and much, much more." She climbed over the counter much like Adele had and started to undress.

"Yes," said Adele. "I think it's time you put that cock to good use." Taking off her clothes, she giggled.

Robert undressed as well. But then, realizing how dangerous it was for the three of them to be having sex behind the counter at the bread shop during business hours, he made one final wish. "I wish that no one interrupts us all day – except maybe Jillian, if she wants to join in!"

The rose on his finger wilted and blew away in an invisible wind.

Now that all three of them were naked, they fondled one another and otherwise got down to business. "Which one of you first?" asked Robert.

"How about both of us?" said Adele.

Robert did not understand.

"Here, look." Adele got on her hands and knees and told Marian to do the same, on top of her. Once they were stacked like that, Robert could see that he had ready access to both their cunts.

Spitting on his dick for good measure, he slid into Marian's pussy and back out, alternating between her cunt and Adele's. Sometimes, one of the women would beg louder than the other, so he would tend more to her needs for a while. But still he did his best to be fair. He made them both come, twice.

Robert then laid down on his back, letting Marian suck his dick while Adele sat on his face. He licked up along her delicious cunt and buried his face there, hungry for the scent of her. And all the while he felt himself grow even harder as the blonde beauty Marian bobbed her head up and down on his cock.

"My! Such a gorgeous threesome you have here!" It was Jillian's sexy voice calling out over all the action. "I thought no one was in, until I heard all the delicious noise you three are making. Care if I watch a while?" She did not even wait for an answer before sitting herself on the counter, her curvy legs dangling and open. She pulled up her dark skirt and began rubbing her fragrant snatch, masturbating to the action down below.

Not wanting to leave Jillian too much out of the equation, Adele stood up from her squat over Robert's mouth and repositioned herself so that she could lick where Jillian was touching herself.

Tired of sucking, Marian took the opportunity to fill her pussy with Robert's dick. On her knees, she bounced her breasts over his chest as she shuttled her pussy back and forth.

Robert reached up and squeezed those gorgeous tits. He pinched her nipples with his fingers and smiled when she cried out.

"Okay," said Jillian, with Adele still licking her pussy, "all good things must come to an end... that good thing being Robert's cock and balls, and that end being mine." She pushed Adele's face away from her cunt and dropped to the floor, pulling Marian up off of Robert until all four of them were standing. "Watch and learn, ladies."

The next thing Jillian did was to pull her dress up over her voluptuous backside and – leaning against the counter – to poke her hungry ass in Robert's direction. Reaching behind herself, she spread her ass cheeks to reveal her dark private hole. "I want you inside me, Robert."

He happily complied, as Adele and Marian both looked at each other over Jillian's penetrated ass. Although he was new to sex in general, he found this hole to be his favorite. The way Jillian moaned and moved told him he would cum soon, but he held out as long as he could.

As he increased the speed of the ass-fucking Jillian, she called out, "Now, which of you two dirty little sluts want to taste me on his big dick?"

"Me!" shouted pigtailed Adele.

"With or without cream, honey-pie?"

"Ooh! With!" Adele clapped her hands, her eyes glued to the steady thrusting movements of Robert's cock and the way Jillian's asshole flexed in response.

"You heard the lady, baker man! Now, cum in my bum..." Jillian reached underneath herself and slapped at Robert's balls while simultaneously shoving her ass up against him to take his cock in as deep as it would go.

Robert could no longer contain himself. Holding onto both of Jillian's naked and sweaty ass cheeks with his bare hands; he shoved his hot load into the depths of her backside.

"Don't stop!" she cried.

Robert kept going, pounding her asshole and creating a slick concoction that was a mixture of his sperm and her ass juice.

Finally, he pulled out, and Adele was right there, licking his cock and choking it down.

Marian, not to be outdone, pressed her face against Jillian's ass and licked her dribbling anus clean.

As Robert stepped back, he smiled.

Marian and Jillian were now kissing, and Adele was watching with Robert. She leaned over and whispered, "Didn't you wish that no one interrupted us all day?"

"Uh, yes."

"Well then, ladies and gentlemen. This day has just begun!" Adele playfully kicked at Robert's now-limp dick. "Come on, let's go! You're going to have to get hard again if you want the three us to hang around all day. We've got holes to fill, you know."

Robert laughed. He felt another hard-on already on its way.

9 SEEING PAST HER CLOTHES

James MacAble owned a bookshop named "Things You Read." He loved running the place, from acquiring items to sell, to stocking them, to interacting with the customers, and to ringing them up at the cash register. A nerd throughout his life, and a nerd still – at age twenty-seven – James found it difficult to interact with anyone and everyone, unless the topic of books could be used as a social lubricant. Then, he could open up and chit-chat with others.

Because of his awkward nature, James had not had a girlfriend for a number of years, as it was difficult for him to find any woman who was both accepting of his quirky demeanor and attractive enough to satisfy his (perhaps unjustifiably) demanding tastes. But James knew what he wanted and was unwilling to settle for anything less.

One day, he heard the sound of the entry bell and looked up from the order catalogue he was perusing. He then saw, in the ovoid frame of his glasses, a woman too gorgeous to believe. She was like James' picture-perfect dream girl, with her long black hair, pretty wide glasses, and petite body nicely wrapped up in a dark outfit reminiscent of Audrey Hepburn in "Breakfast at Tiffany's."

"G-good afternoon!" called James, more than a little nervous.

The woman said nothing but did nod politely to acknowledge his greeting. She then set to browsing the shelves.

Not willing to let this one go, James walked up to her and performed a quick observation. She was obviously stylish, and she was carrying a shopping bag from a local upscale retailer – already containing a few items – alongside her elegant black purse. Also, based on the way she was looking over the bookshelves, she probably had a particular item in mind.

"May I help you find something?"

"Oh, no. Just looking." She had a delightful lilt to her voice that almost sounded innocent – almost.

"Are you looking for a gift?"

"Why, yes I am! How did you know?"

"Oh, I have my ways." James smiled and offered to show her his collection of art books.

She agreed, and soon they were standing before a small cabinet filled with nicely bound full-color art books. Her eyes seemed immediately drawn to the more racy books in the collection, which James took to be a good sign.

"Is this gift for a man... or a woman?"

"A man."

"A boyfriend?"

"No. Just a friend."

Whew. "What does he like?"

"Women, of course," she said with a giggle. "He's also in the Air Force."

"So he likes planes?"

"I guess."

James then showed her a big hardback book with sexy yet tasteful pictures of stewardesses from the last seventy or so years and across several continents. It was nicely done, and it carried with it a subdued yet pervasive sense of kink.

The woman was quite taken by this art book. She even set down her shopping bag and slung her purse over her shoulder so she could look at it with both hands.

While she looked at the pictures, James looked at her breasts. They were small to middling and of an ivory complexion that was worth dying for.

"How much?" she asked.

"Hmm?" James fought to pull his attention away from her tits and the nipples he could not see.

"How much for this book?"

"Umm... Eighty dollars."

"Shoot. I only like to pay in cash, but I don't have enough on me..."

"I'm sure we can work something out. Perhaps a down payment for now and the rest in a few days?" James realized he was willing to bend over backwards for this woman, and he did not even know her name.

"Will sixty be enough?"

"Absolutely!"

James escorted the woman to the cash register and rang up a partial sale. He then bagged the book and handed it over. "Thank you, Miss...?"

"Marcy. Call me Marcy. And I'll be back in three days with the rest of the money. Promise."

"Thank you, Marcy. Have a good day."

She then turned around and marched her pert little bum out of the door.

Afraid he was going to start drooling, James busied himself with tidying up, only to discover that Marcy had left her bag. So, he set it behind the register and waited, expecting her to return before closing.

She did not, however.

So, he took her bag home with him that night, curious as to what might be inside...

Sitting on the couch in his one-bedroom apartment, James found only three items inside the bag. The first was a small silver chain bracelet, the second was a gift card worth forty dollars, and the third was a very strange magazine. More like a brochure than anything else, the magazine consisted of articles on X-Ray Vision, which it spelled in all caps on the cover, just like that. Under the title was a picture of a woman wearing glasses, looking startled and naked, with words in bright pink print that said things like:

-Know what's inside before you buy!
-Is her pushup bra lying to you?
-How skintight is skintight?
-Who's got the biggest wallet?
-Never be fooled again!

The magazine seemed surprisingly legitimate, even though it was all about X-Ray Specs that supposedly really worked. There was even an order form in the back, promising a working pair of glasses with next-day delivery for no more than one hundred dollars in total. There was even a guarantee at the bottom.

Excited at the prospect of such a device, James grabbed his phone and dialed the number. On the other end was an automated system. It congratulated him on his decision and then asked for his credit card number and address of delivery. Not even considering the possibility it was a scam, James gave his number and the address of his bookshop.

There was a moment of silence as the X-Ray Specs computer processed his order, after which the computer said (in halting English): "Yuar Ecks-Ray Specks will be shipped to-morrow. They will arrive the next day. Thank you very much! Goodbye."

Now James had only to wait one-and-a-half days before he would find out whether or not he had been played the fool by Marcy's intriguing magazine.

The next day, James manned his shop and wondered: If he saw a pretty woman looking at his books, what would she look like if he could only see past her clothes? Would he be able to see smooth thighs, round ass, hard nipples on plump tits, or even the furry slit between her legs? How would the lighting work? How would the device know how deep to peer with its X-Ray capabilities?

The more he thought about it, the crazier it seemed... and the hornier he became.

But still, none of the customers, clothed or stripped naked in his imagination, could hold a candle to the fire of his passion for Marcy. She was the one he wanted to see naked, and no one else. At least not yet.

Either way, he had one more day to wait....

On the day Marcy was scheduled to return with the remaining twenty dollars, a delivery boy walked in and dropped down a package on the table next to the cash register. "Sign here," he said.

James did as he was instructed.

The boy left without another word, leaving James alone to inspect and open the package.

It was remarkably simple and straightforward. A box wrapped in brown paper, with a printed label addressing it to James MacAble at "Things You Read" and no return address – just a stamped black silhouette of glasses. Inside was no return receipt or anything of the kind – just a pair of unremarkable glasses very similar to the set already adorning James' puzzled face.

"Well," he said, pulling his normal glasses off and donning his new X-Ray Specs, "no time like the present."

He blinked in quiet surprise. He could see fine through the specs, meaning they corrected his nearsightedness just as well as – if not better than – his regular glasses. "Wow."

Then, he was shocked to discover that the X-Ray quality of these new glasses was for real! All he did was think about seeing through the first row of books, and he did! He could see the row behind. Even more amazing was his ability to fine-tune his depth of vision with nothing more than a mental expression of desire.

Beaming now, he stood behind the cash register, waiting for the first customer to walk into the store, who just so happened to be...

"Marcy!" James waved. "Good to see you!"

"Good to see you, too, James."

Not wishing to wait another second,

James silently commanded his X-Ray Specs to see past the white sundress Marcy was wearing. Instantly, he saw her standing in the middle of the store wearing nothing more than white cotton panties and a matching bra. Her tummy looked deliciously smooth, and her thighs simply begged to be spread wide.

"Oh, yeah. So, here's the last twenty."

James had to wrestle his eyes away from Marcy's beautiful body.

"And, say, did I happen to leave a bag here?" She held a twenty-dollar bill up for James to grab.

"You certainly did, Marcy. I have it right here." Fumbling about in his excitement, he bent down to grab the bag. As he handed it to her, he stared at her waist, noticing a cute little mole on her left hip.

"Are you all right, James?"

"Yes, I'm...." He wished to see past her panties, and what he saw there sent him for a serious tailspin.

Written in black marker, just behind the waistband of her girlish panties, was the phrase "FUCK ME HERE, JAMES!" There was also an arrow pointing down to her shaved pussy, now visible behind the crotch panel of her underwear.

"Uh..."

"Is that all you have to say, James?"

"I..."

"...need..."

"...to..."

"...f-fuck..."

"...me, James. Fuck me." Checking to be sure the store was empty of other shoppers, Marcy pulled James by the hand into the back room.

Finally beginning to adjust to this remarkable situation, James slapped Marcy on her ass before he undid his tie and started unbuttoning his shirt. He laughed as he watched Marcy undress from clothes he could no longer see.

"Take those off, now, James. I'll show you everything you need to see."

He did as instructed and then kissed her hard on the lips. Pulling away to look into her eyes, he said, "So, you planned all this?"

"Yes, James. Believe it or not, I've had my eye on you for quite a little while."

"Why?"

"Let's just say I know one of your former girlfriends, and she told me some bedtime secrets I need to confirm."

James took off his shirt and pants. Then, he stepped up close and personal to the now beautifully naked Marcy.

She looked down with disapproval.

"What? Not big enough?"

"Oh no, that's huge." She pointed her chin lower.

"Oh!" He took off his socks.

"Thank you." She spun around, saying as she turned, "And to reward you for being such a decent booklover...." She raised up her pert little ass, all creamy white and round.

He touched her there, feeling his dick go harder than it had in a very long time.

"Here, let me help you." Marcy reached back and pulled her tight ass cheeks high and to the sides, revealing her pink little anus right above her quivering cunt. "Your choice, darlin'."

James smiled. Marcy had been talking to his previous girlfriend! He pressed her up against the storage room wall and grabbed her by the hips.

He then pulled her onto his cock so that she was forced to support herself with her arms pushed against the wall.

Her cunt, already wet, slid down over his shaft like a hungry mouth trying to get to the end of a long piece of pasta. She moaned, pushing herself even deeper onto his cock.

Because James' hands were so long, he was able to hold her up while at the same time spread her ass cheeks with his thumbs. Pumping her hard, he kept her little red asshole in view, knowing that was where he was going to dump his load.

Marcy obviously loved having her ass stretched wide. She practically screamed with ecstasy.

James gave her a good hard shafting for at least ten minutes. Then, he set her down on the concrete floor, waving his dick with one hand in her direction.

As if entranced by his snake dance, Marcy crawled over to his feet and raised herself up on her knees to stare at the movements of his cock. It glistened with her pussy juice, and she wanted to taste it. Only, when she started to bring her lips toward his dick, he did not agree to the bargain.

Instead, he grabbed her by the hair with his other hand and slapped her face with his cock. Hard. The sound of skin smacking against skin turned both of them on, so he continued to abuse her face until she opened her mouth and begged.

He then presented his cock before her lips, waiting for her to take that first lick.

She did. Then, she did again... and again until she was fluttering her tongue all about the head of his cock.

He grunted in satisfaction and then guided his dick – all of it – into her mouth and down her throat.

She coughed and almost gagged, but then relaxed, letting her spit pour over his balls; afterward, he began to thrust his cock.

Giving Marcy a good throat fucking was only the beginning. When James felt that she had had enough, he pulled back, letting her gasp for air. Then, he pushed her over onto her hands and knees.

"How do you want me, James?"

"I want that cute little asshole up as high in the air as you can lift it."

Pressing her face against the cold

concrete floor, Marcy arched her back and offered up the ass.

"Now, that's how I like it." James rubbed Marcy's spit all over his cock, adding his own to the mix, before he prodded his big dick up against the pink doorbell on her back door. With tiny stabs as her backside, he eventually got her tight sphincter to flex around the wide head of his cock.

Her ass ate it up, and when he pulled back out, she gasped.

"Oh! James, fuck my ass! Fuck it good and hard!"

With one fluid motion, he sank his dick past her widened anus and deep into her rectum. He filled her so well that the underside of his cock managed to press up against and massage her pussy's G-spot.

This was the kind of ass fucking guaranteed to go down in history books!

More than she had when she had wanted to give him a blowjob, Marcy begged and begged for James to keep fucking her. She wanted his cock like a train in a mountain tunnel. She wanted the hot, wet friction of a long stiff shaft exploring every crevice of her girlish rear.

And that is exactly what she got, for a good fifteen solid minutes, until James clutched her ass cheeks with his hands and shuddered, pumping his warm load all up in her ass. And even after he had come in her back door, James continued to fuck her.

Finally, when they were both spent, they fell to the floor, curled in each other's arms, with the fresh smell of anal scenting the air of the bookshop storage unit.

Marcy would no doubt be James' next girlfriend, one he hoped to hold onto for a very long time.

10 SECRET SEX LIBRARY

Ace was a journalist in a world of media. Even before the Virtual Displacement of 2025, the Earth had become so media-saturated that it was difficult to distinguish fact from fiction. Now, in 2028, it was common for a person to live out their entire life in a convincing game environment, only needing to connect with the real world – called the Realer Real – when it was required for safety or financial reasons. Ace's job was to research stories on the link between the Realer Real and other constructed realities that might in some way infringe upon of the lives of the Controllers: those select few human beings chosen to be the caretakers of the Earth.

Ace was a Controller himself of sorts – one that dug up important issues of the day. And today was all about sex. Well, not just sex, really, but a unique sexual application. According to his sources, Ace had learned that a coup was starting in the Brothel Realms of New Sirion, and that virtual sexual encounters were being used to transmit critical (and encrypted) data.

Trouble was, the Brothel Realms of New Sirion seemed to be more rumor than fact, even in the virtual world. This forced Ace to attempt to locate a gateway in the only place he considered reliable: the Library of Secrets. Getting past the library's secure firewall was next to impossible, but Ace had an in. With a specially designed cloaking program, he would appear to be a typical library patron, which should get him closer to his digital prey.

After phasing into the foyer of the Library of Secrets, Ace marveled. The wide, long room had a floor made of marble and walls of mahogany. Spiral staircases, leading up into ethereal static, shifted and swirled all around.

They were fluctuating passages leading deeper (or higher) into the library.

In the middle of all of this, a petite Asian librarian stood on a short pedestal, ready to assist anyone in need. Her black, silken hair hung low in front and high in back, and her smooth, pretty face was adorned with nothing more than a thick pair of round glasses with black plastic frames. The white and blue jacket she wore looked like something a sailor might wear. It was open at the front, revealing her pale, amply bosomed chest to be covered in nothing more than a skimpy, black bra. Below the jacket, she had on a raised, almost horizontal fluffy white skirt, revealing nicely curved thighs that dipped into high black vinyl boots. If Ace looked just right, he could even catch a glimpse of her thin pink panties pulled over her sex and tucked between her round little ass cheeks.

Her name was Suko, and Ace always looked forward to seeing her whenever he was called to research in the Library of Secrets. They had little more than a passing acquaintance, but Ace often fantasized about how wonderful it would be to get to know her better. A whole lot better. Like, with his dick in her tight little Asian twat better.

Ace shook away his lustful thoughts. Checking to be sure he didn't have a hard-on pressed against his blue jeans, he walked across the marble floor and approached the lovely Suko. "Hey there!"

She smiled with her hand raised in front of her mouth, almost blushing. "Greetings, Ace-san!"

"Isn't it about lunch-time?"

"Hai!" she said, in Japanese. "Close enough." Taking this as her cue, she motioned in the air with her hand, summoning her digital stand-in.

Suddenly, there was two of her: one a programmed holographic copy, and the other the real deal. Although even that was a lie, because she and Ace were both just virtual representations of their physical selves. Still, due to the rules of the Library of Secrets, their virtual selves had to abide by most normal physical laws. They could not fly or anything.

Stepping off her pedestal, Suko was surprised to find Ace taking her arm to help her down. She blush a full and sexy red.

"Sorry," he apologized. "I just thought you could use a little help."

"Thank you, Ace-san." She then led the way to one of the moving staircases, which they ascended to their destination.

Ace knew where they were going. Sort of. See, ever since the first time he had visited the Library of Secrets, he had an arrangement with Suko. He would be in need of a private study room, and she knew where the best were hidden. She said she liked to use them on her lunch breaks. Of course, her lunch breaks happened for the most part anytime she wanted, as her virtual body did not require food.

What she really did on her lunch breaks, Ace did not know. All he did know was that she would escort him to a private room hidden behind an array of bookshelves, and then disappear down the aisles to some unknown place on her own. Her business was really none of his legitimate concern, but he was certainly curious.

Only this time, he had other plans. He wanted to follow her, just in case she might be doing something naughty wherever it was she went. After all, considering how sexy she looked, it would only make sense that she might know something about the Brothel Realms of New Sirion.

After sliding open the secret door behind the row of bookshelves, Suko bowed politely and made room for Ace to enter. "Study well, Ace-san," she said.

As Ace entered the secret study room, he noticed again that the top of Suko's head only came up to the middle of his torso, which was wrapped in a casual buttoned business shirt. He couldn't help but imagine how easy it would be to lift her up onto his cock while he was still standing. She could wrap her pretty little legs around his waist and her hands around his neck and bounce, bounce, bounce her tight little pussy on his great big dick.

Once Ace was inside, Suko closed the door.

Inside the study room, which had an interactive research terminal installed in the back, Ace did absolutely nothing before he switched on his cloaking program. Waiting just the few necessary seconds for it to kick in, he then pushed the secret door open again, praying that Suko had walked away... but not too far.

She was not on the other side of the door, and after he stepped back out and closed it again, he was able to hear the soft patter of her booted heels off to the right. Running now, he hurried to catch up with her. Slowing his pace a bit, he walked close to her, but not so close that she might turn and bump into him. After all, thanks to his cloaking program, he was invisible to everyone in the library, Suko included.

It got tricky when she came to a secret door of her own. Past another row of bookshelves, she stopped at a display case. Inside were a number of open picture books and a couple of objects that appeared to be awards of some kind. However, what interested Suko was what was on top of the display case. There she touched an old, discarded book: a small, worn hardback. All she did was twisting it a certain way, and suddenly her virtual representation disappeared!

Ace thought perhaps he had lost her. But then he remembered how she had handled the book and did the same. When he did this, something unlocked, and his reality shifted altogether...

When he found his bearing again, Ace discovered that he was in a large round white room, with pillowed couches as big as beds all throughout its center. In the middle of the room was another raised dais, like the low pedestal Suko used in the foyer to the Library of Secrets – only this dais was about three times as wide and held a small lectern, which stood only three feet high and held a large open book with empty white pages. Next to the lectern and looking at the book, was the ravishing Suko. With her booted legs straight and together, she bent down from her waist, causing her odd little fluffy skirt to lift way up and reveal the way her pink panties barely covered her pussy and her sexy ass at all.

As Ace approached, he did not really care what Suko might be looking at, as he was getting such a great show from behind. He could not help himself. Getting up close to her, he marveled at how smooth and round her ass cheeks were, and at the way her hairless cunt played peekaboo behind her panties. The Brothel Realms of New Sirion could go to hell. He wanted to fuck this beautiful twat. But how, without scaring her?

It was then that Ace's prayers were answered. Suko reached up underneath her skirt to play with her pussy. First she rubbed it through her pink underwear, but as they got soaked from her wetness, she pinched them above her asshole and pulled them back until they slid between her pussy lips. Using her other hand to grab the top front of her panties, she then moved the fabric in a sawing motion up and down the inside of her twat. "Hai! Sooo desu," she moaned, getting herself off.

Ace figured she must be seeing something pretty kinky in her book, but he did not care anymore. He loved watching her masturbate. In fact, it was getting him so hard, that he decided to pull his dick out from their cramped place in his jeans. With a quick unzip, he freed his tremendous erection right then and there. "Ah!"

Suko stopped. "Ace-san? Is that you?" Standing upright once more, she turned around and peered about behind her thick black framed glasses.

Ace was horrified. How could she know?

"It's okay, Ace-san. I know you are here. That's why I put on my little show – just for you." She blinked her beautiful black eyes. "But wouldn't you rather fuck me now?"

"Oh god yes!" he shouted, turning off his cloaking program and throwing caution to the wind.

When Suko saw him appear before her, next to the dais, she smiled. She bent down to get a closer look at his cock. Thinking it more than big enough – maybe even too big – she straightened up again and reached under her skirt. With a quick tearing motion, she ripped her wet panties off her body altogether. Then she leapt up onto Ace's chest and lowered herself, oh so carefully, onto his monstrous cock.

Its bulging head was a little wide for Suko's pussy lips, so she reached down and spread them open, helping her tight twat to swallow down the thick tip of his dick. After that initial positioning, the rest of him slid in even easier as she sat down on the full length of it.

With both her hands laced behind Ace's neck now, Suko bounced and bounced, just like he had always fantasized her doing. Looking at her face, surrounded by her midnight hair, he loved the glasses. They made her seem like a slutty schoolgirl who made herself blind from looking at pictures of cock.

But now she had the real thing.

Grabbing her ass cheeks, he spread them wide and thrust in rhythm with her bouncing. Then he set her down and took off his clothes.

She did the same, even setting aside her glasses on the lectern.

Now they were ready for some serious fucking.

But first Suko took his dick in her mouth. Tasting her own pussy juices, she slobbered all over him, taking him deep down her throat. Barely able to breath and choking from the sheer size of his cock, Suko proved to be a real trooper. Although Ace did not believe it to be possible, she made him even harder than he had been the first time.

Then he sat down on the dais, and

had Suko sit on top of him, facing away and leaning forward. Her tight twat swallowed up his super-hard shaft and she bounced her pert little butt over and over, taking all of it in repeatedly. He could even feel her smack up against his balls; she took him in so deeply.

Wrapping his arms around her, he fondled her hefty tits, squeezing her nipples between his fingers and jiggling the weight of her breasts like he had found the perfect new toy. But what was even better was the cunt on his cock.

When Suko reached down between her legs and cupped his balls in her hand, Ace could not hold out any longer.

"Oh, god!!!" Cum shot up in Suko's cunt, dripping out all along the shaft of his mighty penis and balls.

Finally, Suko got up and turned around. She then licked him clean of cum; sucking and kissing him from his balls to the tip of his dick, letting him lose his hardness and rest a bit.

Eventually, Ace realized he had neglected his journalistic mission, only to discover that Suko was indeed involved with the Brothel Realms of New Sirion, and that she was intent on recruiting him over to their side.

He did not put up much of a fight, looking forward to joining their ranks and fucking Suko on a regular basis.

AUTHOR'S NOTE

Readers: I want to expand a few of the stories to see where the characters can be explored further. If there are any of the stories that you would like to read more about again, I'd love to hear from you!

Visit my blog at www.garrettzeiger.com

Join my newsletter for free exclusive previews
www.garrettzeiger.com/in

Follow me on Twitter at
http://www.twitter.com/garrettzeiger

Like my page on Facebook at
www.facebook.com/garrettzeiger

Discover my books at major ebook retailers everywhere.